Neddie to the Rescue!

Betsy raised the window and lowered Neddie onto the roof.

"Hold on to my hand," said Betsy. "Pick up the bird with your other hand. Don't let go."

Neddie felt the roof under his feet but the snow was deeper than he thought it would be. He stretched out his arm to pick up the cardinal. Suddenly, Betsy's father called out, "What are you doing up there?"

Neddie was so surprised that his foot slipped and he let go of Betsy's hand.

Betsy, Star, and Susan watched with their mouths open as Neddie slid right off the roof! To their great surprise, they saw the cardinal, a streak of bright red, fly into a nearby tree. Betsy's father saw Neddie coming. He opened his arms and caught him as he dropped off the roof. Then they both toppled into a big snow-drift!

Snowbound with Betsy

Carolyn Haywood

AN ARCHWAY PAPERBACK
Published by POCKET BOOKS • NEW YORK

An Archway Paperback published by
POCKET BOOKS, a Simon & Schuster division of
GULF & WESTERN CORPORATION
1230 Avenue of the Americas, New York, N.Y. 10020

Published by arrangement with William Morrow and Company, Inc.
Library of Congress Catalog Card Number: 62-10656

ISBN: 0-671-56048-4

First Pocket Books printing December, 1980

10 9 8 7 6 5 4 3 2

AN ARCHWAY PAPERBACK and colophon are trademarks
of Simon & Schuster.

Printed in the U.S.A.

IL 3+

To
Margie (*g* as in *gay*) Esherick

CONTENTS

Chapter 1

Old Mother Hawkins is Picking Her Geese

Betsy was nine years old the year the big blizzard came just before Christmas. Betsy's sister Star was only three, and Betsy said Star was so little that she probably would not remember about the blizzard when she was grown up. Betsy said *she* would never forget it, because of everything that came with the blizzard.

The day the great snowstorm began was very much like every school day for Betsy. When she got up, she found that the morning was cold. The sky looked grayish-white and so heavy it seemed ready to fall down at any minute. Soon she started off to school, bundled up in her warm snow pants and her bright red jacket with a hood. She was wearing the hood over her head. It kept her ears warm, but her nose felt very cold. Every once in a while, Betsy covered her nose with her mitten to warm it up. Her feet were cold too, but she didn't know any way to warm her feet, except to get to school as fast as she could. Betsy hurried. Part of the way she ran.

When she turned the last corner and saw Mr. Kilpatrick's red police car, Betsy knew she did not have to go much farther. Mr. Kilpatrick was the policeman who saw the children across the big, wide street where the buses went back and forth to town. All the children loved Mr. Kilpatrick. He knew most of their names. He had called Betsy "Little Red Ribbons" ever since she had been in the first grade.

One day when she had lost her way Mr. Kilpatrick had taken her to school in his car. Since then she had ridden in Mr. Kilpatrick's red car many times, and the policeman had become an old friend.

Mr. Kilpatrick was always ready to joke with the children. This made him a very special friend of Billy Porter's. Billy and Betsy had been friends ever since they met in the first grade. They often went to school together and played at each other's houses.

This morning Mr. Kilpatrick was wearing his ear muffs to keep his ears warm, his thick gloves to keep his hands warm, and his galoshes to keep his feet warm. Betsy caught up to a group of children on the corner. They were waiting for Mr. Kilpatrick to stop the traffic, so that they could cross the big, wide street.

"Hi, Betsy!" Billy Porter called out when he saw her. "Look, I'm a dragon! Look at the smoke coming out of my mouth!" Billy held his breath and then breathed out into the cold air. "I'm a dragon!" he repeated.

"That isn't smoke," said Betsy. "It's just your warm breath hitting the cold air. Everybody is doing it."

3

"We're all dragons!" cried Kenny Roberts.

All the children began to blow into the air. "We're dragons!" they shouted. "We're dragons!"

"Mr. Kilpatrick is the biggest dragon!" cried Billy, pointing to the puffs of mist that were blowing out of the policeman's nose and mouth.

All the children began to shout, "Mr. Kilpatrick's a dragon! Mr. Kilpatrick's a dragon!"

Mr. Kilpatrick held up his big hand and blew his whistle. The cars and a big bus stopped. Then he turned his head toward the children, and with a big smile he waved to them to cross the street. "What is all this racket about?" he said, when the bunch of children reached him.

"Look, Mr. Kilpatrick!" cried Billy. "Look at our breath. We're all dragons!"

"Well, get along with you," said Mr. Kilpatrick with a chuckle, "and stop draggin' your feet." And he laughed his big laugh.

The children ran, laughing, to the other side of the street. Betsy turned to wave her hand to Mr. Kilpatrick, but he had already turned away and the traffic was whizzing

by. Mr. Kilpatrick was hidden by a passing bus. "Mr. Kilpatrick is so funny!" said Betsy to Billy.

"Yes," replied Billy, laughing. "Mr. Kilpatrick said, 'Stop draggin' your feet!' "

Betsy and Billy went the rest of the short way to school together. Billy puffed and sang, over and over, "I'm a dragon! And I'm draggin' my feet."

When they reached the schoolyard, the lines of children were forming to go into the building. Miss Richards, one of the teachers, was directing the ihildren. When she saw Billy, she said, "Billy Porter, lift your feet."

"I'm a dragon! Puff! I'm draggin' my feet," said Billy.

"Don't say *draggin'*, Billy," said Miss Richards. "Say *dragging*."

"Dragging," said Billy.

When the children reached their classroom, Billy said to Betsy, "Miss Richards spoiled it. She spoiled Mr. Kilpatrick's joke."

"Well, teachers have to teach you how to talk," said Betsy. "Mr. Kilpatrick doesn't have to teach us how to talk. He takes us across the street."

"Well, when I grow up, I'm not going

to be a teacher," said Billy. "I'm going to be a policeman."

"I'm going to be a teacher," said Betsy.

"I'll have more fun being a policeman," said Billy, as the class was called to order.

Just before the bell rang for school to be over, it began to snow. Billy was the first one to notice it. "It's snowing!" he called out.

Every child looked out the windows. They all felt excited. In that part of the country it was not often that there was snow before Christmas. They could hardly wait for the bell that ended school to ring.

Finally the bell rang, and Betsy and Billy started off together. They lived in the same direction, and often walked home with each other. "It's beginning to snow hard now," said Betsy, as they stepped out the door.

"Sure is," replied Billy, "and tomorrow is Saturday! We can go sledding."

Soon Betsy and Billy reached Mr. Kilpatrick's corner. A group of children were waiting to cross the street. Mr. Kilpatrick beckoned to the children, and they hurried forward in a bunch.

When they reached the policeman, Billy called out, "It's snowing, Mr. Kilpatrick!"

"That's right!" said Mr. Kilpatrick. "My grandmother in Ireland used to say, whenever it snowed, 'Now Old Mother Hawkins is picking her geese.'" The children laughed as Mr. Kilpatrick crossed the street with them.

When they reached the pavement, Betsy said, "I don't think the snowflakes look like feathers, Mr. Kilpatrick. They are beautiful little designs. Look!" Betsy held out her arm and Mr. Kilpatrick and Billy looked at the snowflakes on the sleeve of Betsy's red jacket.

"They're pretty, aren't they?" said Mr. Kilpatrick.

"Nobody could ever make a snowflake so perfect, could they?" said Billy.

"No," replied Betsy. "They just make themselves, coming through the air."

"You don't say!" said Mr. Kilpatrick. "And here I've been thinkin', all these years since I was just a bit of a lad, that they were goose feathers."

Betsy and Billy laughed and looked up into Mr. Kilpatrick's twinkling eyes. "I guess you never made a snowball, Mr. Kilpatrick," said Billy. "You can't make a snowball out of feathers."

8

"You can't build a snowman out of feathers, either," said Betsy.

"Sure! You have no idea what they can do where I come from," said Mr. Kilpatrick. Then he blew his whistle for the traffic to change.

Betsy and Billy went on, but they turned around to look back at Mr. Kilpatrick. They saw him laughing.

As the children walked on, Betsy said, "Oh, Billy! Maybe the snow will last for Christmas!"

"That would be great!" said Billy. "We could go sledding every day all through the holidays."

"Christmas is soon," said Betsy.

"Yepper!" said Billy. "Next week."

When they reached the corner, the children saw something that was a sure sign of Christmas. A big truck was parked beside the curb and two men were unloading Christmas trees from it. A heavy rope was stretched along the curb between two telephone poles.

Betsy sniffed the odor of the evergreen trees. "Smells like Christmas!" she said.

The children stopped beside the truck to look at the Christmas trees. They were tied together in bundles. One of the men was in the truck. He was throwing the bundles of trees out of the back of the truck. The other man lifted the bundles over the rope and cut the strings that bound the trees together. As the trees separated, the man stood them along the sidewalk, resting them against the thick rope.

Billy went to the back of the truck and looked up at the load of Christmas trees. "There are some big ones on this truck!" he shouted to Betsy, who was standing on the sidewalk.

"Out of the way, sonny!" the man on the truck called to Billy. Billy moved aside as the man threw the bundle of trees down to his helper. "Wonder where Bob is," he said, as he tossed them down. "He promised to come over to help us."

"I don't know," said the other man. "Sure wish he would come. I want a cup of coffee."

"Me too," said the man on the truck. "I'm nearly frozen stiff."

"The diner is right across the street," said the other man, as he cut the string on the bundle. "We could keep an eye on the truck."

"I'll watch it for you while you get a cup of coffee," said Billy.

"You will?" said the man, looking up.

"Sure!" replied Billy.

"Hey, Harry!" the man called up to the man in the truck. "This little fellow says he'll watch the truck while we get a cup of coffee."

"And I'll watch the trees for you," said Betsy.

"Okay!" said Harry. "We won't be more than a minute." He scrambled down out of the truck. "Come on, Ray," he said to the other man. "Let's get the coffee."

"This snow sure is coming down," said Ray. "If it keeps up all night, there's going to be a lot of snow on these trees in the morning."

"Never mind the weather, Ray," said Harry. "Let's get the coffee while we have helpers."

The two men crossed the street and went into the diner. Betsy and Billy were alone with the Christmas trees. "I'll stay here behind the truck," said Billy. "You stay there on the sidewalk with the Christmas trees."

"What shall I do if someone comes along and wants to buy one?" Betsy called back.

"Sell it to him," said Billy.

"But I don't know how much they are," said Betsy, sticking her head betwee two trees that were leaning against the rope.

At that very moment, the rope that was holding up the trees came untied from one of the poles, and all of the Christmas trees fell with a swish into the street. The avalanche of Christmas trees knocked Billy over and buried him.

Billy called out, "Hey! Help!" Betsy ran to help him.

Christmas trees seemed to be everywhere. They looked much bigger lying in the street than they had standing along the sidewalk. Betsy thought she had better run over to the diner and call Harry and Ray. While she was waiting for the traffic to go by, she saw Mr. Kilpatrick's red car coming down the street. Betsy jumped up and down and waved for Mr. Kilpatrick to stop. The red car slowed down and stopped beside Betsy.

"What's the matter, Little Red Ribbons?" Mr. Kilpatrick called out.

"Billy's under the Christmas tree!" Betsy called back.

"Under the Christmas tree!" exclaimed Mr. Kilpatrick. "It's pretty early to be

finding things under the Christmas Tree,"
he added, as he stepped out of his car.

Betsy led Mr. Kilpatrick to the spot
where Billy was thrashing around under
the branches of a big spruce tree. "Well,
I never!" said Mr. Kilpatrick, lifting some
of the branches. When he saw Billy's
frightened face, he said, "Look what's under the Christmas tree!"

Billy crawled out. He knew that he had
not been hurt, but just scared. "Thanks,
Mr. Kilpatrick," said Billy, dusting spruce
needles off himself.

"Are you all right?" asked the policeman.

"I'm all right," replied Billy. "I just
didn't know what hit me at first."

Just then Harry and Ray came running
across the street from the diner. When they
saw all the Christmas trees lying in the
street, they said, "What happened?"

"The rope gave way," said Betsy. "The
Christmas trees fell over on Billy."

"That's right!" said Mr. Kilpatrick.
"Billy was under the Christmas tree and
Santa Claus didn't put him there."

"Oh, that's too bad!" said Harry. "Are
you okay?"

"Oh, sure!" Billy replied.

"Look," said Harry, "here are a couple of little trees. One for each of you. You can have them for taking care of the place for us." Harry picked up two little trees. "Can you carry these?"

"Oh, yes!" said Betsy. "Thank you!"

"You bet!" said Billy. "Thanks a lot."

"Here," said Mr. Kilpatrick, "I'll run you both home. Throw those trees into my car. I'm through for the day." Harry threw the trees into the back of Mr. Kilpatrick's car and the two children climbed into the front seat.

As they drove away, Betsy and Billy called out to Harry and Ray, "Have a Merry Christmas! Thanks for the Christmas trees!"

Chapter 2

A Midnight Surprise

When Betsy reached home, she carried her little Christmas tree through the front gate and around the house to the back door. She leaned the tree against the house beside the door. Then she opened the back door and stepped into the kitchen.

Betsy's mother and her little sister Star were in the kitchen. Betsy smelled a delicious odor. Her mother was taking a pan of Christmas cookies out of the oven. "Hello, Mother!" said Betsy. "It's snowing! Mr. Kilpatrick brought me home in his red car. And I have a Christmas tree!"

"You have!" exclaimed Mother. "Where did you get a Christmas tree?"

"It's just a little bit of a one," replied Betsy. "Come, look out the back door."

Mother opened the door. Star was right beside her. She wanted to see the Christmas tree, too. Mother and Star peeked out, but before Mother could close the door, a great gust of wind blew snowflakes into the kitchen. With the snowflakes came Thumpy, Betsy's cocker spaniel. Snow was sticking to his back and hanging from the feathers on his legs. His muzzle was white with snow. Thumpy shook himself, and the snow that was all over Thumpy flew all over the kitchen.

"Now look!" said Betsy's mother. "Look what Thumpy has done!"

Betsy laughed. "I'll get the mop," she said. "I'll mop it up."

"That will be a help," said her mother.

"What do you think of my Christmas tree?" asked Betsy.

"It's a nice little tree," replied her mother. "It is very tiny, but it will look just right on the table in the hall."

"Father will get a big one for the living room, won't he?" said Betsy.

"Yes, indeed!" replied Mother.

While Betsy mopped the floor, she told her mother about Billy and the Christmas trees.

When Betsy had finished her story, Mother said, "Did Mr. Kilpatrick have any trouble driving his car in this snowstorm?"

"He had to drive slowly," Betsy replied, "because the streets were slippery."

"It was very kind of Mr. Kilpatrick to bring you home," said her mother. "I'll be glad when Father gets home."

"Did Father take the car today?" asked Betsy.

"Yes, he did," her mother replied, "and he had a long trip to make." Mother sounded a little bit worried. Then, more to herself than to the children, she said, "He will be all right. He has the turnpike most of the way, and we are only a few miles from the turnpike. He'll be all right."

Both Star and Betsy helped to decorate the cookies. They trimmed some with pink sugar and some with green sugar. They sprinkled tiny, brightly colored balls on others. When they were all baked, there were hundreds of cookies. "They are a lot of cookies!" said Betsy, looking at the cookies spread out all around the kitchen.

"Yes," replied her mother. "I'm going to give a lot of them away as little Christmas gifts."

"How many days until Christmas, Mother?" Star asked.

Mother looked at the calendar hanging on the wall. "Seven, just one week," she said. "I hope this snowstorm won't keep me from going to the city to do some Christmas shopping tomorrow."

"May we go, too?" asked Betsy. "Tomorrow is Saturday."

"To see Santa Claus?" said Star.

"We shall have to see what kind of day it is tomorrow," replied Mother. Then she added, "I do hope Father won't be late for dinner."

"Come, Star," said Betsy, "let's watch for Father at the front window." The children went into the living room. It was dark and Betsy turned on one of the lamps. The

children stood at the window, watching for their father's car to turn into the drive. The bright headlights on each passing car showed the falling snow. The cars drove very slowly.

While the children watched at the window, Mother browned some cubes of beef to make a beef stew. Then she peeled some potatoes and scraped some carrots. When she peeled the onions, tears came into her eyes. As she put the meat and vegetables into a baking dish, she wondered how near home Father was. While the dinner was cooking in the oven, Mother sat in the living room with the children. She hemmed a dress for Star.

After a while, Mother looked at her wrist watch. It was six o'clock. It was time to take the dinner out of the oven. Mother went into the kitchen. Soon she called the children from the window to have their dinner.

After Mother had served the children, she placed the baking dish back in the oven to keep it warm. "Aren't you going to eat your dinner, Mother?" Betsy asked.

"I'll wait for Father," Mother replied.

"I guess Father will be glad to get some

of this dinner," said Betsy, "with all this good gravy and these dumplings."

"Well, there is plenty of it," said Mother, laughing. "If we are snowed in, we can eat beef stew all week. And there is plenty of rice pudding, too."

When the children had finished their rice pudding, Mother washed the dishes while Betsy dried them. Star and Thumpy lay beside each other on the rug in front of the open fire in the living room. Star colored pictures in a book with her crayons. Thumpy snored.

When the dishes were finished, Betsy curled up in a big chair by the fire and read a book. Mother sat by the window, straining her ears for the sound of Father's car, but all she heard was the sound of the back wheels of a car, squealing as they spun round and round. "Someone is stuck!" said Mother.

"Is it Father?" asked Star.

"No," replied Mother, looking out of the window. "It isn't Father."

Betsy and Star soon went upstairs with their mother. It was time for the children to go to bed. Mother gave Star a bath and tucked her into the lower berth of the bunk beds that were in Star's room. Betsy had twin beds in her room. When Betsy came out of the bathroom, she jumped into her bed and pulled up the covers. Her mother came in and kissed her good night. Then she opened the window a crack. "I'll just open the window a wee bit," said Mother. "We don't want the window sill covered with snow in the morning."

"I wish Father would come home," said Betsy. "Do you hear that wind, Mother?"

"Yes, I do," replied Mother, "but go to sleep now. Father should be here soon."

"Aren't you hungry, Mother?" Betsy asked.

"I'll have something when I go downstairs," replied her mother.

But when her mother went into the kitchen, she didn't want anything to eat. She went back to the living room and turned on the radio. A man was speaking about the weather. He said that high winds had turned the storm into a blizzard, that cars were stuck on all the roads, and that everyone should stay indoors unless they had an emergency. Betsy's mother turned off the radio and picked up a book. She tried to read, but she kept listening. She began to hear cracking noises. Once or twice the sound was like a shot from a gun. She listened, wondering what the sounds could be. She put another log on the fire. It was very cozy and warm. Soon Mother fell asleep.

When she woke up the room was dark, except for the embers that glowed in the fireplace. She wondered who had turned out the light. She reached over and pushed the button on the lamp beside the chair. Nothing happened. The room stayed dark. Mother got up and went to the door. She flicked the wall switch. There was no light. By the light of the embers, Mother turned the knob on the radio. There was no light in the dial and no voice spoke to her. Then she knew that something had happened to the electricity.

Mother went to the fireplace and, leaning over, she looked at her watch to see what time it was. To her great surprise, it was quarter past twelve. Midnight! she thought. And Father isn't home yet! Just then she heard a sound like the ones that she had heard earlier in the evening. It was like a shot. Suddenly she knew what it was. The noise was made by branches and limbs breaking from the trees. "The snow must be terribly heavy to break the branches off the trees," she said to herself.

Suddenly Thumpy gave a little bark. Then he ran to the front door. Just as Mother got up to follow Thumpy, she heard the sound of a key turning in the lock. Before she reached the door, it was thrown open.

There, framed in the doorway, stood Betsy's father, and the only reason Mother could see him in the dark was because he was white with snow. To Mother's surprise, Father was carrying something white over his shoulder. It looked like a heavy sack of potatoes. "Oh!" cried Mother. "I am so glad to see you!"

Father laughed. "I have brought some guests," he said, stepping aside. A woman holding a small traveling bag in one hand and a little girl by the other hand came into the hall. Snow clung to their clothes in heavy wads. As Father stepped through the door, he said to Mother, "This is Mrs. Byrd, dear, and Susan. This fellow over my shoulder is Neddie." By this time there was snow all over the hall carpet, but Mother was so glad to see Father she

didn't care. Father placed Neddie in a chair. He was still fast asleep.

"My car broke down on the turnpike," said Mrs. Byrd. "Your husband has been so kind to us. I don't know what we should have done without him."

"My car didn't break down, but it's stuck," said Father. "Fortunately both cars are near the exit. I found the Byrds trudging along just ahead of me."

Mother helped Mrs. Byrd take off the children's snow suits, while Father lit the candles that were on the mantel over the fireplace. "I kept hoping that you would telephone," said Mother to Father.

"I tried to call you," said Father, "but the wires are down and the telephones have been knocked out."

"You must all be starved," said Mother. "I have beef stew in the oven, and there is plenty of it. Go sit by the fire while I get it for you."

Father put two logs on the fire while Mother went out into the kitchen. Neddie lolled in the big chair by the fire, as limp as a rag doll. "Shouldn't you wake him and give him something hot to eat?" asked Betsy's father.

"I'll try," said Neddie's mother. But

she couldn't wake Neddie. Susan stood in front of the fire, warming her hands. The firelight made her red hair shine like copper.

Soon Mother came into the room with a tray. On the tray were some warm plates, the covered baking dish, and a wicker basket piled high with crisp brown rolls. When Mother lifted the lid of the baking dish, the stew was smoking hot. "I am so glad nothing has happened to the gas stove," said Mother. "At least I can cook."

"And we have plenty of wood for the fireplace," said Father.

Just then Neddie opened his eyes a crack. Then he rubbed them with his fists. When they were open, he said, "I'm hungry!"

"Well, Neddie!" said his mother. "Here is a wonderful dinner for you."

Neddie looked at the flames leaping in the fireplace. Then he looked up at the candles. He turned his head and looked at the strange room in the dim light. "Where are we?" he asked.

"We are with friends," said his mother. "Very kind friends."

"Are we going to stay here?" asked Neddie.

"You certainly are," said Betsy's mother. "We have two little girls. Star will be three on Christmas Day."

"I'm six," Neddie interrupted.

"And Betsy is a little bit bigger than Susan," said Mother.

"I'm eight," said Susan.

"Star has bunk beds in her room," said Mother, "and there are twin beds in Betsy's room."

"Where will Mommy sleep?" asked Susan.

"There is a little bed in the sewing room," said Betsy's mother. "She will be quite comfortable there."

Everyone ate the beef stew, and it tasted better than anything they had ever eaten before. When they all had cleared their plates, Father said to Mrs. Byrd, "Don't worry about your car."

"I'll try not to," said Mrs. Byrd. "I just wish I could telephone my mother and my husband."

"Well, that isn't possible tonight," said Father, "with the telephone service in such a bad state."

"Perhaps things will be better in the morning," said Mrs. Byrd, as Betsy's mother led her and the two children up-stairs.

Susan and Neddie went to bed quietly. It all seemed very mysterious to them, going to bed in a strange house in the dark. Star didn't so much as stir in the lower bunk when Neddie climbed into the upper. Susan crawled into the other bed in Betsy's room while Betsy slept peacefully. Soon everyone in the house was asleep. The fury of the storm was shut out, and the rattling of the windows did not waken anyone the rest of the night.

In the morning Betsy woke up facing the window. She opened her eyes and saw that the snow was still falling. Snow was stuck all around the edges of the windowpanes. Betsy could see the limbs of a big tree heavy with snow. Gusts of wind blew the snow from the roof across the window. It looked as though someone were waving white silk scarves across it. Betsy pushed her feet way down under the warm covers. She lay still and listened to the wind. Then she heard the scrape of a shovel. Someone was shoveling snow.

In a few minutes, Betsy rolled over so that she faced the other bed. She was surprised to see a hump in the middle of the bed beside her. She wondered what was making the hump. She sat up and looked at it more carefully. Her eyes followed the hump to the pillow. There was some red hair spread out on the pillow. Betsy got up and leaned over the bed. Then she saw that there was a little girl in the bed. A little girl she had never seen before. A little girl with freckles on her nose. She was sound asleep. Betsy felt terribly excited. She knew now how the baby bear felt when he discovered Goldilocks asleep in his bed.

Without stopping to close the window, Betsy slipped into her bathrobe and slippers. She went out into the hall and listened at the head of the stairs. She could hear her mother rattling pots and pans in the kitchen. Betsy ran downstairs and into the kitchen. Her eyes were very big as she said, "Mother, there is a little girl in the other bed in my room, and I never saw her before in all my life."

Before her mother could answer, Star burst into the kitchen. "Mother!" she cried. "There is a little boy hanging upside down out of the top of my bed!"

Mother laughed. "Yes!" she said. "We have company, Neddie and Susan. Their mother is here, too. Father brought them all home with him last night. They had to walk for miles through this terrible storm."

"Oh, the poor things!" exclaimed Betsy. "Where is their mother?"

"She is outside helping your father knock the snow and ice off the trees and bushes," replied her mother.

"Oh!" cried Star. "Now we have somebody to play with! Somebody to play with!"

Chapter 3

Neddie Byrd Rescues a Bird

Betsy and Star were very excited over their unexpected guests. They went upstairs to take another look at their roommates. "Come into my room, Betsy," said Star. "Come see!"

Betsy followed Star into her room, but instead of a little boy hanging from the upper bunk, they found Neddie hanging over the window sill. The window was wide open, and Betsy thought he was about to fall out. Snow was blowing all around him. "Neddie!" Betsy cried, as she rushed across the room. Neddie pulled himself back, dragging snow from the window sill with him. He stood shivering in his pajamas. Betsy pulled the window down. "Neddie!" she cried. "Don't you know there is a blizzard? You could freeze yourself, hanging out of the window."

Neddie's teeth were chattering, but he said, "B-b-but th-th-there's a b-b-bird."

"Here!" said Betsy, pulling the quilt off Star's bed. "You'd better get warm." Betsy wrapped the quilt all around Neddie and shoved him into Star's bed.

Just then Susan came into the room. She was wearing a blue bathrobe. "Hello!" she said.

"Hello!" said Betsy.

"Are you Betsy?" asked Susan.

"Yes," replied Betsy, "and this is Star."

"Hello, Star!" said Susan.

"Hi!" said Star. "Neddie had the window open."

"There was a bird, Susan," said Neddie. "It flew against the window and made an awful bang. A red bird. It's on the porch roof, under the window. I saw it, but I couldn't reach it."

Susan and Betsy and Star went to the window to look out. Star was too little to see anything, and Susan and Betsy couldn't see much.

"You have to open the window," said Neddie. "You can't see it if you don't open the window."

"Open the window, Betsy," said Star.

"We can't open the window in a blizzard," said Betsy.

"Maybe the bird has hurt its wing," said Susan. "If it can't fly, it will freeze out there in the snow."

"Oh, dear!" said Betsy. "If it's a red bird, I guess it's a cardinal."

"It will freeze!" said Neddie, joining the girls at the window.

"We'd all better get dressed right away," said Betsy. "We can't do anything about the bird until we get dressed." Betsy helped Star to dress. While Susan and Neddie were dressing, they ran back and forth from one room to the other, talking about the bird. Neddie saw a hot-water bottle hanging on a hook in the bathroom, and he thought it would be a good idea to

drop it out to the bird. "It's bad enough that the bird dropped itself," said Betsy, "without dropping a hot-water bottle on it."

"We could let it down on a string," said Neddie. "It would keep it warm until after breakfast."

"No!" said Betsy. "No hot-water bottle!"

When the children were dressed in their warmest clothes, they met again at the window in Star's room. "We can't leave the poor bird on the roof," said Susan.

"Let's see if it's still there," said Neddie. "Let's open the window, Betsy."

"But it's so cold!" said Betsy. "And the snow comes in."

"Just enough so I can stick my head out," said Neddie.

"Well, all right," said Betsy, "but be quick." Betsy raised the window sash. The biting cold air blew in. "Now hurry!" said Betsy.

Neddie stuck his head and shoulders out of the open window. He raised himself on his toes and looked down. "He's there!" he shouted. "I can see his red feathers."

"Let me see!" cried Star.

"Let me see!" Susan cried.

"The snow is coming in," said Betsy. "Come in, Neddie. I have to shut the window." Neddie pulled himself inside and Betsy shut the window.

Just then Betsy's mother called upstairs, "Come to breakfast, children."

Betsy and Star ran to the head of the stairs. "Oh, Mother!" Betsy called down. "There is a wounded bird down on the porch roof. We have to rescue it. It's a cardinal! Please wait, Mother."

"Your cocoa will have skin on top," said Mother. "And the corn muffins will be dried out."

"Oh, but what about the cardinal?" said Betsy. "We have to be kind to animals."

"Whatever you are doing," replied Mother, "please do it quickly."

Betsy and Star went back into Star's room. "We have to hurry up and think of a way to get the bird," said Betsy. "It must be nearly frozen, and anyway, breakfast is ready."

"There is only one way to reach it that I can think of," said Susan.

"How?" cried the other children in a chorus.

"Why, climb out on the roof and pick it up," replied Susan.

"In the blizzard!" exclaimed Betsy. "Who is going to climb out on the roof in all this snow?"

"Oh, I could climb out," said Neddie.

Betsy thought about this for a moment, and then she said, "I guess you could if I help you. I am the biggest and I could hold on to you, but you must be quick about it."

"I don't need anybody to hold on to me," said Neddie.

"But the snow is deep and the porch roof isn't as near this window as it looks," said Betsy.

"I can get that bird easy," said Neddie.

"You will have to put on your snow suit," said Susan.

"Okay!" said Neddie.

The four children dashed down the stairs to the hall closet. Star called out to her mother, "Mother! Neddie is going to get the little bird." Her mother didn't hear her. She was busy shoveling snow away from the back door.

Susan helped Neddie put on his snow suit. Meanwhile, Betsy put on her coat and pulled the hood over her head. Then they all traipsed back to Star's room.

Suddenly Neddie sat down on a chair, and said, "I don't want to pick up the bird."

"Neddie!" cried Betsy. "I thought you wanted to do it."

"Think of the little bird out there in the cold," said Susan. "You must do it, Neddie."

"Well, I want to do it," said Neddie. "I want to climb out on the roof, but I never picked up a bird before. Maybe I won't like the way it feels."

"Don't be silly, Neddie!" said Betsy. "You will like picking it up. Please, Neddie! Our cocoa is getting skin on top."

"And the muffins are getting hard," said Susan.

"You have your mittens on," said Betsy. "You just have to pick it up with your mittens."

"Think how important you are," said Susan, "rescuing a cardinal in a terrible blizzard."

"Maybe you will get your picture in the paper," said Betsy.

Neddie thought about this. Then he said, "There isn't anybody to take my picture."

"Neddie!" exclaimed Susan. "Are you going to save that little bird's life or aren't you?"

"All right," said Neddie, getting up from the chair. "I'll do it."

"Now," said Betsy to Susan and Star, "you must go out of the room, because it will be terribly cold with the window open."

"Oh!" cried the girls together. "How can we see?" said Susan.

"Want to watch," said Star.

"You can watch from the window in my room," said Betsy. "You can see fine from there."

Susan and Star ran into Betsy's room and went to the window that looked out over the porch. Star climbed on a chair in front of the window. From the window, Susan and Star could see Betsy's father and Mrs. Byrd out in the snow. They were trying to knock some of the snow and ice off the evergreen trees with brooms. They were standing in snow up to their knees. Gusts of wind were blowing the snow into great drifts. Right in front of the porch there was a high drift.

Soon Star and Susan heard the window being raised in Star's room. They saw

Neddie's feet and legs come out of the window. Then they saw all of Neddie being lowered down onto the roof.

"Oh! It's deep!" they heard him say.

"Hold on to my hand, Neddie," said Betsy. "Pick up the bird with your other hand. Don't let go."

Susan knocked on the window, and shouted, "Be careful, Neddie! Pick it up gently!"

"Don't fall!" shouted Star. They watched Neddie sink deeper and deeper into the snow.

Betsy's father stopped knocking the snow off the trees and looked up to see why the children were knocking on the windowpane. When he saw Neddie on the roof, he trudged through the deep snow to the porch.

Now Neddie felt the roof under his feet, but the snow was deeper than he had thought it would be. The cardinal lay very near the surface in a pocket of soft snow. Neddie leaned over. His right hand held on to Betsy's. He stretched out his left arm to pick the bird. Suddenly, just as Neddie had the bird in his hand, he heard Betsy's father call out, "What are you doing up there?"

Neddie was so surprised that his foot slipped and he let go of Betsy's hand.

Betsy, Susan, and Star all shouted, "Be careful, Neddie!" as they saw Neddie sit down in the snow.

Then, with a swish, Neddie slid.

"Oh! There goes Neddie!" Star shouted.

Betsy, Star, and Susan watched with their mouths open as Neddie slid right off the roof. Then to their great surprise, they saw the cardinal, a streak of bright red, fly into a nearby tree. Betsy's father saw Neddie coming. He opened his arms and caught Neddie as he dropped off the roof. They both toppled over into a big snowdrift. When they had pulled themselves out of the snow, Neddie said, "Oh! I lost the bird!"

All of the excitement was over now, and everyone sat down to breakfast. The children didn't mind having skin on their cocoa, and nobody cared about the muffins being a little bit hard. Everyone was very hungry. "We must put some food out for the birds," said Betsy.

"Yes," said Susan. "We must be kind to animals."

"Sure!" said Neddie. "And I hope I

have to rescue another bird from the roof. That was more fun than sledding.''

"One rescue like that is enough!" said his mother. Everyone laughed.

"Cheer! Cheer! Cheer!" chirped a cardinal outside the dining-room window. "Cheer! Cheer! Cheer!"

Chapter 4

Popcorn

Betsy and Star and their unexpected play-
mates didn't care how hard it snowed. The
more it snowed, the more snow there
would be to play in. Susan and Neddie's
mother did care how much it snowed, be-

cause it kept the telephone men from repairing the damage and getting the telephones working again. She could not telephone to the children's father, whom they had left the morning before, and she could not telephone to their grandmother, who was expecting them for the week end.

Outside, the wind blew the snow into great drifts. One drift was piled up against the garage door. Only half of the picket fence in front of the house showed above the snow. Broken electric wires hung from the poles and were caught in the trees. They crackled as blue sparks shot out of them like Fourth of July sparklers. No cars passed the house. The morning paper didn't come. The milkman didn't come. The mailman didn't come. Just more and more snow came.

There was even too much snow for Thumpy, who loved snow. Whenever it snowed, he ran to the door to go out as soon as anyone said the word *snow*. On the hottest day in the summer, no one could say *snow* without throwing Thumpy into a fit of squealing at the door. Now Thumpy would only venture out as far as the clearing from the back door to the garbage can.

The children stood at the windows in the living room. "I wish we could go out in the snow," said Neddie. "I'd like to see how deep it is. I'll bet it's up above my knees."

"I guess Star wouldn't be able to walk in it at all," said Susan.

"Mother says we can't go out until it stops snowing," said Betsy.

"When it stops we can make angels in the snow," said Susan.

"Angels in the snow!" exclaimed Betsy. "I've made snowmen in the snow, but I've never made angels."

"Is it like angel cake?" Star asked.

Susan laughed. "No, Star, it isn't like angel cake."

"What is it like?" said Star.

"I'll show you when we go outside," said Susan.

"You never told me about angels in the snow," said Neddie. "I don't believe you know how to make angels in the snow."

"Yes, I do!" said Susan. "But I'm not going to tell you."

"Let's look at television," said Betsy. "My favorite program is on every Saturday morning. It's puppets."

"Oh, my favorite program is Saturday

morning, too," said Neddie. "It's Roly from Polyland."

"I want to see the puppets," said Star.

"I don't like puppets," said Neddie. "I want to see Roly."

Star began to cry. "I don't want to see any old Roly. I want to see the puppets."

"Star!" said Betsy. "Susan and Neddie are our company. You must always do what the company wants to do."

"Goody!" said Neddie. "We're going to see Roly from Polyland!"

"I think we should draw straws," said Susan. "That would be fair."

"Soda-pop straws?" said Star. "Are we going to have soda pop?"

"Oh, no, Star!" said Betsy. "Not that kind of straw."

"What kind of straws?" said Star.

"Long ones and short ones," said Neddie. "And the long one wins. Doesn't the long one win, Susan?"

"Yes, the long one wins," replied Susan.

"But we haven't any straws," said Betsy.

"Don't you have a broom?" Susan asked.

"Oh, yes, of course!" said Betsy. She

went into the kitchen and came back with her mother's broom. "Here, Neddie," said Betsy, "you pull one out."

Neddie took hold of one straw and pulled. He held it up in his hand.

Betsy turned to Star. "Now, Star, you pull one," she said. Star was delighted to pull a straw out of the broom, but she couldn't make up her mind which straw she wanted to pull. "Hurry up, Star!" said Betsy. "It's almost time for the program." Star finally settled on the straw she wanted to pull. She pulled and she pulled, but her tiny fingers couldn't make the straw come out of the broom. "Here, I'll pull it for you," said Betsy. "You're not strong enough."

Betsy pulled out a straw, but Star cried out, "That isn't the one I wanted to pull." Betsy held up the straw.

Neddie saw at once that it was longer than the one he had pulled. "No fair!" cried Neddie. "You pulled the wrong one. We have to do it over again."

"Neddie!" said Susan. "You should be ashamed. You haven't any manners!"

"Never mind!" said Betsy. "It's time to turn it on. We'll look at Roly."

Neddie looked a little bit ashamed, and

53

said, "We can look at half of Roly and half of the puppet show."

"Very well," said Betsy, as she pulled the button out to turn on the television. The four children sat down on the floor to watch the program. They waited for the picture and the sound. Nothing happened. "It takes a little while for it to warm up," said Betsy.

"Ours warms up quicker than that," said Neddie.

Betsy got up and twisted the dials on the left side. Then she twisted the dials on the right side. The screen remained a solid, dark, dull green. "That's funny," said Betsy.

"It's broken," said Neddie.

"Oh!" cried Betsy. "It's the blizzard! I forgot about the blizzard. There isn't any electricity."

"Oh, dear," sighed Neddie. "No Roly from Polyland."

"And no puppets," said Susan.

"What shall we do now?" said Star.

"Let's do something that doesn't take so long to start doing it," said Neddie.

"Maybe we could pop popcorn," said Betsy. "We just got a new popper."

"Oh, that would be fun," said Neddie. "Then can we eat it?"

"Of course!" Betsy replied

"I love popcorn," said Susan.

"We have a big can of corn for popping," said Betsy. "It's in the pantry closet." Betsy led the way to the pantry closet. The other children followed. In the kitchen, Betsy opened the pantry-closet door and picked up the lower part of the corn popper. "Here, Susan," she said, "you take this part."

Then Betsy picked up the glass dish and lid. "I'll carry that," said Neddie.

"No, you'd better carry the can of corn," said Betsy. "You might drop the dish and break it."

"I never drop anything," said Neddie.

"Well, you'd better let me carry the dish," said Betsy. "You carry the can."

"All right," said Neddie. "But I never drop anything." Neddie took the big can from Betsy. He held it in both arms. "Where shall I take it?" he asked.

"Oh, we can make the popcorn in the living room, in front of the fireplace," said Betsy. "Take it into the living room."

"What can I carry?" Star asked.

"You can carry this lid," said Betsy,

handing the lid of the popping dish to Star. "Carry it in both hands."

The parade of children moved toward the living room. Neddie, with the big can of corn, led the way. Just as he reached the entrance to the living room, he tripped over the rug. He tried to keep from falling, but he began to stumble. Neddie stumbled and stumbled and stumbled across the living room until he was stopped by a large armchair. Then the can flew out of his arms and the lid fell off. There was a shower of corn. A whole pile of corn spilled into the seat of the armchair, and corn flew all over the living room.

"Oh, Neddie!" cried Susan.

"Somebody tripped me!" said Neddie.

"Look at the corn!" cried Betsy.

The children stood speechless, looking at the carpet, the chairs, and the tables. There was corn everywhere. Corn had even flown into the fireplace, where it soon began to pop. As it popped, it flew back into the room. Star picked up a piece that had flown back from the fireplace. She held it out to Betsy. "Look, Betsy!" she said. "Popcorn!"

While Betsy looked around at the corn, Susan was looking at the popcorn popper.

There was a long black cord hanging from it. "Betsy!" said Susan. "This popper is an electric corn popper!"

"Oh, dear!" Betsy cried. "I forgot about that. I forgot that it's electric."

"Everything is electric," said Susan.

"And just look at all this corn that we have to gather up," said Betsy.

"Better get the vacuum cleaner," said Neddie.

"The vacuum cleaner is electric," said Susan.

"We can't waste all this corn," said Betsy. "We can't waste anything when we're having a blizzard. If our food runs out we may have to live on it for days."

"You mean we're going to eat popcorn that's been on the floor?" asked Susan.

"It will be dirty," said Neddie.

"We can wash it and dry it," said Betsy. "Then it will be clean enough to use." Betsy left the room and returned with two big spoons, a little shovel, and a whisk broom. "Here!" she said. "Everybody help put the popcorn back into the can."

The children crawled around the room, gathering up the corn from the floor and off the furniture. Every once in a while a kernel popped in the fireplace, and a little white rosette flew up the chimney or out into the room. The air began to be filled with the odor of burned corn.

After a while Betsy's mother called downstairs, "I smell something burning. What is it I smell?"

"It's popcorn," Betsy called back.

"Oh, are you popping corn?" her mother replied.

"No, Mother," Betsy called again, "not really."

"Then what do I smell?" said her mother.

"They are just sort of little samples," said Betsy.

When all the corn that the children could find was back in the can, Betsy carried it to the kitchen. She poured the corn into a colander and sprayed water on it.

"Are you going to put soap flakes in?" Neddie asked.

"Oh, no!" cried Betsy. "Just water."

"Do we have to dry every piece, one at a time?" Neddie asked. "Like knives and forks?"

Betsy and Susan laughed. "It would take us until next year!" said Betsy.

"It's an awful lot of work," said Neddie. "And we can't pop it when we get through, because the popper is electric and we don't have any electricity."

"We can pop it when we get some electricity," said Betsy.

"Why don't you put all this corn on a cooky tin in the oven?" said Susan. "It would dry in the oven."

"That's a good idea, Susan," said Betsy. "The cooky tins are in the closet beside the stove. You get one for me." Susan opened the closet door and took out a cooky tin. "Maybe we had better have two cooky tins," said Betsy. "There is a lot of corn here." Susan brought the two cooky tins to the counter beside the sink. Betsy emptied the corn out of the colander onto the two tins. When she had finished, the cooky tins were piled high with corn. "I think it will dry nicely," said Betsy, as she placed the cooky tins in the oven.

"It's too bad we haven't any electricity," said Neddie. "I would love to have some popcorn."

"We have a popper at home," said Susan. "It's sort of a cage on a long pole. You put the corn in it and shake it over the fire in the fireplace."

The children went back into the living room. Star picked up a book and brought

it to Betsy. "Betsy," said Star, "please read a story."

"All right," said Betsy. "Does everybody want to hear a story?" Everybody wanted to hear a story, so Betsy opened the book and began to read. Soon the children were lost in the land of make-believe. Everything else was forgotten. They forgot the snowstorm, the television, the popcorn popper, and the corn in the oven.

After a while Betsy's mother came downstairs. It was almost lunch time. "I can still smell popcorn," said Betsy's mother.

Popcorn! That one word brought Betsy back from the land of make-believe with a rush. She dropped the book and ran to the kitchen stove. Her mother followed her. Betsy opened the oven door, and a shower of fluffy, white popcorn spilled out. The whole oven was filled with popcorn. It looked as though someone had shoveled the snow into the oven.

When Betsy's mother saw it, she cried, "Betsy! Whatever made you do that?"

"I didn't mean to pop it," said Betsy. "I only meant to dry it."

"Dry it!" exclaimed her mother. "What do you mean, dry it?"

"It was so wet," said Betsy.

"Wet!" said her mother. "How did it get wet?"

"When we washed it," replied Betsy.

"But why were you washing it?" her mother asked.

"Because it was so dirty, from being on the floor and everything," said Betsy.

"Well, none of this makes any sense to me," said her mother. "But one thing is certain, we must empty the oven of all this popcorn."

"That's a lot of popcorn," said Neddie. "I just love popcorn!"

"I'm glad you do," said Betsy's mother, "because every bucket and can in the house is going to be filled with popcorn."

Chapter 5

Something for the Birds

On Sunday morning Betsy woke up early. She saw at once that the blizzard was over. The sun was shining, and it seemed to be shining more brightly than ever before. Betsy got up and looked out the window. The sun shone on the snow and made it so bright that Betsy had to squint her eyes. The ice-covered trees and bushes sparkled with tiny rainbows. The rainbow colors were fire bright. A cardinal lighted upon a branch of a bush. Betsy wondered whether it was the cardinal that Neddie had gone out the window to rescue. The bird was the brightest red she had ever seen. On the ice-covered branch, he was as bright as the red glass birds that hung on the Christmas tree every year. Now a pheasant appeared. A beautiful cock stepped from between two bushes.

Betsy called to Susan, who was still asleep. "Susan!" she called. "Come quick!"

Susan woke up and rubbed her eyes. "What's the matter?" she asked.

"Come see the pheasant!" said Betsy. "He's beautiful!" Susan jumped out of bed and ran to the window. "See!" said Betsy. "He's pecking at the low branches. I wonder whether he is finding anything to eat!"

"Just ice, I guess," said Susan.

"It's terribly cold to eat ice," said Betsy.

"We should make a birds' Christmas tree," said Susan, "and trim it with food for the birds."

"Like what?" Betsy asked.

"Pieces of suet are good," said Susan.

"I don't think my mother has any suet,"

said Betsy. "But we have all that popcorn. Do you think birds like popcorn?"

"Maybe," said Susan. "I know that pheasants like corn, so maybe they like popcorn, too."

Betsy was still watching the pheasant. "I wish I could walk on top of the snow the way that pheasant does," she said. "But I would sink right in up above my knees."

Neddie came running into Betsy's room in his pajamas. "What are you doing?" he asked.

"Look at the pheasant, Neddie," said Betsy.

"Oh, isn't it pretty!" said Neddie, looking out the window.

"We're going to make a Christmas tree for the birds," said Betsy. "We can use that nice little tree that is out beside the back door. The man who sells Christmas trees gave it to me."

"What will we hang on the tree?" Neddie asked. "Balls and candy canes?"

"No, of course not!" said Betsy. "What would the birds do with balls and candy canes? We have to hang food on the tree."

"Birds are just crazy about peanut butter," said Susan.

"How are we going to hang peanut butter on a tree?" exclaimed Betsy.

"Peanut-butter sandwiches?" cried Neddie. "Whoever heard of a Christmas tree with peanut-butter sandwiches hanging from it?"

"Not peanut-butter sandwiches, Neddie," said Susan. "Just peanut butter."

"Well, I don't know how you can hang peanut butter on a tree," said Betsy.

"You have to put it in something," said Susan.

"Like what?" Betsy asked.

"Well, I know somebody who put food for the birds in a half of a coconut shell. Then she hung it up," said Susan.

"A coconut shell!" exclaimed Betsy. "I'm sure my mother doesn't have any coconut shells. She buys coconut in boxes."

Star came into Betsy's room in her nightgown with her clothes in her arms. She heard the word *coconut*. "I want some coconut!" she said.

"Coconut is for the birds," said Neddie.

"No, Neddie!" said Susan. "The coconut isn't for the birds. The coconut shell held the food for the birds!"

Just then Betsy's mother called up the

stairs. "Come, children! Breakfast will soon be ready."

Neddie scampered back to Star's room. Susan ran into the bathroom and turned on the water. Betsy and Star began to dress. Betsy helped Star with her buttons. Soon the four children were washed and dressed. They ran down the stairs and into the kitchen. "Good morning!" they shouted.

"Good morning!" replied their mothers. Mrs. Byrd was helping Betsy's mother prepare the breakfast. Mrs. Byrd was pouring orange juice from the squeezer into a glass. Seven full glasses stood on the kitchen table. They were surrounded with orange skins.

Susan picked up one of the orange skins. "Look, Betsy!" she cried. "We could hang these on the tree!"

"Orange skins!" cried Star. "Don't want orange skins on the Christmas tree!"

"For the birds, Star!" said Susan. "We can make little baskets and put peanut butter in them."

"Oh, that's wonderful!" cried Betsy. "It's just the thing!" Then she added, "Mother, we're going to trim a Christmas tree for the birds."

70

"That is nice for the birds," said her mother, "but we have only one jar of peanut butter. Either there is peanut butter for your sandwiches or peanut butter for the birds. You children will have to decide which it will be."

"I love peanut-butter sandwiches," said Star in a sorry voice.

"So do I," sighed Neddie.

"But the poor little birds are hungry," said Susan.

"I'm hungry," said Star.

"Me, too!" said Neddie. "I would like to have a peanut-butter sandwich for breakfast."

"You are having cereal," said his mother. "All of you, sit down and eat your breakfast."

"Please don't throw away the orange skins, Mother," said Susan.

"They are all here," replied her mother. "All twenty-eight halves."

"That's wonderful!" said Betsy. "But we should have more than that."

"First we have to vote about the peanut butter," said Susan, as she sat down at the table.

"Yes!" said Betsy, pulling up her chair. She looked around the table and said, "All in favor of giving the peanut butter to the birds, hold up your hand.''

"Betsy, Susan, and Neddie held up their hands. Star just looked into her bowl of cereal.

"Star," said Betsy, "we'll let you help trim the tree for the birds." Star kept right on looking into her bowl of cereal.

Betsy's father came into the room. "Good morning!" he said, as he sat down at the head of the table.

"Good morning!" the children and their mothers replied.

"Now," said Betsy, "I'll ask the question again. All in favor, hold up your hand." This time all the children raised their hands. Betsy's father raised his hand, too. Betsy laughed and said, "Why, Father! You don't know what you're voting for."

"I know I don't," her father replied. "I just like to vote for things. Now tell me, what did I vote for?"

"To give up peanut butter for the birds," said Betsy.

"Good!" said her father. "I don't like the stuff anyway. It sticks to the roof of my mouth. Are you sure birds like peanut butter?"

"They love it!" said Susan.

"I'm glad I voted in favor of it," said Father.

"We just have to get more orange skins!" said Susan. "Twenty-eight won't be enough to trim the tree."

Betsy's eyes brightened with an idea. "I guess," she said, "if we went over to the Jacksons' right after breakfast, we could get their orange skins. They always have orange juice for breakfast. There is Mr. Jackson and Mrs. Jackson, and Clementine, who cooks, and Lillybell. Lillybell," Betsy explained to Susan and Neddie, "is Clementine's little girl."

"Lillybell is my friend," said Star.

"They have two oranges apiece every morning," said Betsy, "so that's eight oranges, and each one cut in half makes sixteen skins."

"Oh, that's wonderful!" said Susan.

"Then there are Mr. and Mrs. Robinson, across the street from the Jacksons. We can get eight more orange skins there," said Betsy. "We still need more, but they would help."

"Isn't there somebody with five or six children?" Susan asked.

Betsy thought a moment. "Not right around here."

"The snow is so deep," said Susan. "Can we walk to the Jacksons' in this deep snow?"

"No," said Betsy. "I guess Father will have to pull us on our sled."

"What's that?" said Father, who had been busy talking to Mrs. Byrd about her car.

"Will you pull us on our sled, Father?" asked Betsy. "So that we can get the orange skins?"

"Orange skins!" exclaimed her father. "Do you mean that you are asking me to pull you around on a sled, while you collect the neighbors' garbage?"

"But Father, it's for the birds," said Betsy. "You voted in favor."

"I voted in favor of giving them the peanut butter," replied her father. "I did not vote for orange skins."

"But you see, Father," said Betsy, "we can't give the peanut butter to the birds unless we have orange skins."

"Why not?" said Father.

"Because we have to serve the peanut butter to the birds in the orange skins," Betsy explained.

"Served in orange skins!" exclaimed her father. "And I suppose you are planning to give them napkins and finger bowls?"

All the children laughed merrily over this. Then Betsy said, "You see, Father, you can't put peanut butter on trees without putting it in something."

"I know that," her father replied, "but I am not going out to collect garbage for the birds!"

"I wish you wouldn't call it *garbage,* Father," said Betsy. "It's just orange skins."

"An orange skin without the orange inside is garbage," said her father. "If you want to hang *our* garbage on a Christmas tree, very well. But I will not have the neighborhood garbage hanging on the Christmas tree."

"All right," sighed Betsy. "We'll have to use just our orange skins, but they will only trim one side of the tree."

"Well, in such weather as this," said her father, "half a Christmas tree is better than none."

After breakfast Susan and Betsy scraped the inside of the orange skins until they were clean. Then they put some peanut butter into each one. They spent the rest of the morning making little cradles of string to hold the orange cups. The girls set Neddie to work stringing popcorn on a heavy thread. Star sat eating popcorn out of the big can. "We'll put some of the popcorn garlands on the birds' tree, and the rest we can save for our own Christmas tree," said Betsy.

While Betsy and Susan were busy making the tasty ornaments for the birds' tree, Mrs. Byrd was paring apples for applesauce. She pared the skins around and around without breaking them. When she finished, the entire red apple skin lay curled up on the table. When Betsy saw the apple parings, she said, "Oh! We can hang those apple skins on the birds' Christmas tree."

"Oh, yes!" said Susan. "They will hang like icicles."

"Whoever heard of red icicles!" said Neddie, threading his needle through a piece of popcorn.

It wasn't until after lunch that everything was ready to be hung on the tree. The children put on their snow suits, their hoods, and their galoshes. Susan carried the basket with the trimmings for the tree in it to the side porch, and Betsy brought the little Christmas tree from beside the back door. The snow was very deep, and the children

sank so far into it that they could hardly walk. Star fell over every time she tried to take a step. They had to choose a spot for the tree near the house, because they couldn't walk very far in the deep snow. They finally stuck it into the snow close to the dining-room window. The snow held the little tree upright.

"This is a good place for it," said Susan, "because we'll be able to see it from the window."

"Yes," said Betsy. "We'll be able to see the birds eating the peanut butter."

"Lucky birds!" said Neddie. "They get all the peanut butter."

"I love peanut butter," said Star, longingly.

Susan and Betsy hung the orange cups on the branches of the tree. Neddie helped to hang the apple parings. Finally Betsy and Susan draped several garlands of popcorn from branch to branch, all the way from the top to the bottom of the tree. When they were finished, the children were very pleased with the birds' Christmas tree. They stood and admired it. The bright orange cups against the dark green branches made the tree very gay.

"It looks like a real Christmas tree," said Susan.

"I'll bet the birds will be very pleased," said Betsy.

"I hope they appreciate our peanut butter," said Neddie.

Betsy's father came out and looked at the tree. "Isn't it a beautiful Christmas tree, Father?" said Betsy.

"Well," said Father, "it certainly is different! It's the only Garbage tree I have ever seen."

Chapter 6

Candles for a Birthday Cake

Late Sunday afternoon the snowplow went past Betsy's house. It was the first thing that had gone by for two days. It threw the snow into great piles on each side of the street. After it passed, more snow than ever blocked the driveway. Now that the street had been opened up, Betsy's father said he didn't feel so cut off from the rest of the world. For about the hundredth time, Mrs. Byrd said that she wished she could telephone to Susan and Neddie's father and grandmother.

"The phone will surely be working by tomorrow morning," said Betsy's father.

"I certainly hope so!" said Mrs. Byrd. "They must both be very worried about us."

"I wish we had some more candles," said Betsy's mother. "We have used up all the candles. There are none left but birthday-cake candles."

"We can't burn birthday-cake candles without a birthday cake," said Betsy.

"If it were Christmas, it would be my birthday," said Star. "Then we would have a birthday cake with candles."

"Couldn't we celebrate Star's birthday today?" Neddie asked. "Then we could light the candles."

"I don't think candles on a birthday cake would give us much light," said Mrs. Byrd.

"Will we all sit in the dark tonight?" asked Susan.

"Oh, don't worry. We shall have the light from the fireplace," said Betsy's father. "It's a good thing we have plenty of firewood."

"I wonder how Mr. and Mrs. Jackson are getting along," said Betsy.

"And Clementine and Lillybell," said her mother.

"Suppose you children put your things on," said Father. "Now that the street is plowed, I believe we can walk over to the Jacksons' and see how they are."

"That's a good idea," said Betsy's mother. "Mrs. Byrd and I will fix some supper while you're gone."

"Do we still have plenty of food, Mother?" Betsy asked.

"Yes, in the freezer," her mother replied. "But if the electricity doesn't come back soon, it will all be defrosted."

"Oh!" cried Betsy. "Then all the ice cream in the freezer will melt!"

"If the electricity doesn't come on soon," said her father, "we shall have to build an igloo and put the food in it."

"What's an igloo?" asked Neddie.

Betsy answered Neddie's question. "The Eskimos live in igloos," she said. "They are houses built of ice and snow."

"I'd like to play in an igloo," said Neddie, as he pulled up the zipper on his jacket.

"Come along, children! Hurry up!" said Betsy's father, as he pulled Star's galoshes on over her shoes.

At last all the children were ready to set forth. "Good-by! Good-by!" they called to their mothers, as they went out the front door.

The children walked along the path that had been cleared to the front gate. Father followed them. Snow fell off the tree in front of the house as they walked under it. Snow fell off the gate when Betsy opened it. Outside the gate, the children found themselves in deep snow. The sidewalks had not yet been cleared, and a great bank of snow separated them from the street.

"We'll have to walk in the street," said Father. "I'll help you children over this bank of snow." Father stepped into the snowbank. His whole leg disappeared. One by one, he lifted the children over the pile of snow and set them down in the street. Several cars had been parked by the curb. The snowplow had almost buried them.

Susan stood looking at the cars. She pointed to one of them and said, "I guess Daddy's car out on the turnpike looks just like that car."

"Daddy's car and my car must have been towed away by the police by now," said Betsy's father.

"Won't we ever get it back?" asked Susan.

"Oh my, yes!" said Father. "I shall probably get a notice in the mail tomorrow telling me where my car is."

"And will we get a notice?" Susan asked.

"Your father will get one," said Betsy's father, "because he is the owner of the car. They always notify the owner."

"Daddy still won't know where we are," said Susan.

"No, but he will have some idea of where you are," replied Father.

When the group reached the corner, they stopped to watch the linemen, who were putting the telephone wires back where they belonged. The men called down to the group below, "Hi, down there! Watch out for the wires if you're going for a walk."

"Okay!" the children called back.

"When can my mommy telephone to my daddy?" Neddie called up to the men.

"I don't know, sonny," one of the men called back. "We're working as fast as we can. Maybe tomorrow. Things are in a mess."

The children and Father walked on. They turned the corner at the end of the street, and there was the snowplow ahead of them. It was cutting through the snow and piling it up by the sidewalk. They followed the plow around the next corner. As the plow passed the Jacksons' house, Betsy's father said, "There goes a ton of snow into the Jacksons' driveway."

The Jacksons' house was large, with wide steps leading up to a big porch. The porch ran all around the house. No path to the steps had been cleared. "Come here, Star!" said her father. "I'll have to carry you through this snow." Father picked up Star and broke the trail through the smooth drifts.

"Oh! This would be a good place to make angels in the snow!" said Susan.

"We could make an igloo, maybe," said Neddie.

"Come along!" said Father. "We're not stopping to make anything."

Father led the way. His feet made big, deep tracks in the snow. The three children, following him, tried to step in his footsteps, but they found it hard work.

First Neddie fell down, and everybody laughed. Then Betsy fell down, and they all laughed again. Finally Susan fell down, and there was more laughter. By the time they had climbed the snow-covered steps, snow was sticking all over their clothes.

Betsy reached up and pushed the doorbell. She heard it ring inside. In a moment she heard heavy footsteps coming toward the front door. Suddenly the door was jerked open, and there stood Mr. Jackson. "Well," he cried, "if it isn't Betsy! Hello! Come in!"

Father put Star down inside the front door. Then he shook hands with Mr. Jackson. As he did so, he said, "We have brought our visitors." He waved his hand toward Susan and Neddie, and said, "Just a couple of snowbirds—Susan Byrd and Neddie Byrd."

"Come in! Come in!" said Mr. Jackson. "So nice to see you, Susan and Neddie. Take off your things."

As the children were pulling off their snowy clothes, Mrs. Jackson appeared. She kissed Betsy and Star, and said, "I'm so glad to see you. We have been wondering how you were getting along in all this snow."

Betsy introduced Susan and Neddie to Mrs. Jackson, and Mrs. Jackson shook hands with the two children. As they walked into the living room, Betsy said, "We've been getting along fine, and there is still a lot of ice cream in the freezer."

"It's going to be very dark at night," said Susan, "because we don't have any more candles."

"Neither have we," said Mrs. Jackson. "We don't mind sitting in the dark, but Lillybell is heartbroken."

"Where is Lillybell?" asked Star.

"She's in the kitchen, crying," said Mrs. Jackson.

"What is she crying about?" asked Betsy.

"Today is Lillybell's birthday," said Mrs. Jackson. "Clementine made her a beautiful birthday cake, but we haven't any candles to put on it."

"And my car is stuck in the driveway, so there is no way to get the ice cream," said Mr. Jackson.

"We have birthday-cake candles!" said Star.

"And we have loads of ice cream in our freezer," said Betsy.

"If we had known, we would have brought the candles and the ice cream with us," said her father.

"We could have had a birthday party," said Star.

Just then Lillybell came into the room. She was wiping tears from her eyes. "Hello, Lillybell," said Star.

"Hello, Star," Lillybell replied.

"Happy birthday, Lillybell!" said Betsy.

Lillybell sniffled and said, "Thank you."

"Lillybell," said Betsy, "this is Susan and this is Neddie."

Lillybell sniffled again, and said, "Hello." Then she put her arm over her eyes and burst into tears.

Betsy went to Lillybell and put her arm around her. "Don't cry, Lillybell," she said. "We have candles at our house."

Lillybell took her arm down from her face, and said, "Birthday candles?"

"Yes," said Betsy, "birthday candles."

"Are they pink?" asked Lillybell. "I like pink."

"I don't know what color they are, but they are birthday candles," said Betsy.

Soon the children were all in the kitchen

90

looking at Lillybell's cake. Clementine had covered it with pink icing. It stood, big and high, on a white plate. "That's a beautiful birthday cake!" said Susan.

"It isn't a birthday cake unless it has candles," said Lillybell.

"Now, Lillybell!" said her mother. "You just sit down with all these nice children and have yourself a nice birthday party with this nice cake. Your mommy's got more to cry about than you have. Just think what happened to your mommy's best hat. That beautiful hat made of feathers, with that lovely veil with a diamond fastened on it. Just like a dewdrop, it was. Blew straight off my head coming home in that blizzard, and I never did find it again. Just like a bird, it went! Your mommy's got something to cry about, but is she crying? No indeed! She's just grateful her head didn't blow off, too. I never felt such a wind in all my life."

"Oh, Clementine!" exclaimed Betsy. "That was a beautiful hat."

"Yes, 'twas, honey!" said Clementine. "But it's no more! That beautiful hat is just what they say, 'gone with the wind.' I'll never see it again."

"Why don't we take the cake over to our house?" said Betsy's father, coming into the kitchen. "We can put our candles on the cake and have our ice cream."

"Oh! That would be wonderful!" cried Betsy. "We'll have a real birthday party for Lillybell."

Lillybell's eyes grew big and round and her face began to shine. "Would you like that, Lillybell?" asked Betsy.

"Oh, yes!" said Lillybell.

"Well, let's go!" said Betsy's father.

Now five children scrambled into their snow suits. Soon they were on their way, with Father lifting Star and Lillybell over the high piles of snow. Betsy carried the cake in a box. She walked carefully, because she did not want to fall down with the cake.

They were almost home when Susan saw a red police car stop in front of Betsy's house. "There is a police car at your house, Betsy," she said.

"Oh, maybe it's Mr. Kilpatrick!" exclaimed Betsy. Sure enough, Mr. Kilpatrick stepped out of the police car. When he saw the children and Betsy's father, he walked toward them. "Hello, there!" he called out. "Old Mother Hawkins did a good job of picking her geese this time, didn't she?"

Betsy knew what Mr. Kilpatrick meant and she laughed. "Yes, she did," she replied.

"Do you know of any strangers around here by the name of Byrd?" Mr. Kilpatrick asked. "A mother and two children?"

Betsy's mouth dropped open in surprise. "Why! Why!" she said.

But before Betsy could say any more, Susan said, "Our name is Byrd. I'm Susan Byrd and this is my brother Neddie. Our mother is inside."

"Well!" said Mr. Kilpatrick. "Your father will be glad to know where you are. The police have radioed all the way along the turnpike. They have been searching for you in every town along the 'pike."

"Can you radio to our father?" Susan asked.

"I can send the message along," replied Mr. Kilpatrick, "and I'll do it right away."

"Oh, that's wonderful, Mr. Kilpatrick!" said Betsy.

"My mother will be glad," said Susan. "Thank you very much."

Mr. Kilpatrick climbed back into his car.

Just as he was about to start the car, he remembered something. "Oh," he said, "I almost forgot! Do you folks need any candles? The police thought people might be running out of candles, so we're taking them around. I can give you a box."

"We certainly do need candles," said Betsy's father, "and we're very grateful to you."

Mr. Kilpatrick handed out a box of candles, and everyone cried, "Thank you, Mr. Kilpatrick!"

"We don't need any birthday-cake candles," said Star, " 'cause we have some."

"Well, that's a good thing," said Mr. Kilpatrick, "because I haven't any birthday-cake candles with me."

"Do you think the birthday-cake candles are pink, Betsy?" said Lillybell.

"I don't know what color they are," replied Betsy, "but when there is a blizzard you mustn't be too fussy."

As Mr. Kilpatrick waved his hand to the children, Betsy called to him, "Mr. Kilpatrick, Mrs. Jackson needs candles, too!"

Susan had already run into the house, shouting. "Mommy! Mommy! Daddy knows where we are!"

"He does?" cried her mother.

"Well, almost," replied Susan. "Mr. Kilpatrick is sending Daddy word over the police radio!"

"We're very important people, aren't we?" said Neddie, who had just come in.

"Well, we are to Daddy," replied his mother.

Chapter 7

Snowman and Ginger Cookies

On Monday morning there was no sunshine. The sky was heavy and gray again. The electricity was still off, and the telephone was still out of order. The only voice that Betsy could hear from outside came through the little radio that belonged to Betsy's father. It didn't need any wires. Father carried it to the breakfast table. He was waiting for news of the weather. Soon a man on the radio said, "More snow is expected tonight." He continued, "All schools will be closed today."

"Hurrah!" cried Betsy. "No school!"

"We can build a snowman!" cried Neddie.

"Will you help us build a snowman, Father?" asked Betsy.

"Build a snowman!" exclaimed her father. "I have to go to work. I shall have to walk to the station. In this kind of weather I wish I had a dog sled."

"There's Thumpy!" said Betsy, laughing. "Maybe you could hitch Thumpy to my sled."

"I would need a dozen Thumpys to pull me to the station," replied her father, as he leaned over to kiss Betsy good-by. He kissed Star, and patted Susan and Neddie on the head. "See that you build a good snowman, Neddie," he said.

"Okay!" said Neddie.

When the children finished their breakfast, they put on their snow suits and went out into the snow. Thumpy went too.

"Where shall we build the snowman?" said Neddie.

"We mustn't put it near the birds' Christmas tree," said Susan. "We might scare the birds away."

"I think we should build it on the front lawn," said Betsy. "Then everybody who goes past the house can see it."

"I think so, too," said Susan.

The children tramped around from the back door to the front lawn. "Now," said Betsy, "we have to start rolling snowballs. The more you roll them, the bigger they get."

"Is he going to have legs?" asked Neddie.

"Of course he's going to have legs!" said Betsy. "You and Susan can make the legs. I'll make the body."

"Who's going to make the head?" asked Neddie.

"If you make a good leg, Neddie," said Betsy, "you can make the head."

"Shall I make a long leg or a short leg?" asked Neddie.

"Just a medium-sized leg," replied Betsy.

"Okay!" said Neddie, rolling his ball of snow.

Susan and Betsy set to work, too. In a few minutes Betsy looked over at Neddie. "Neddie!" she said. "That isn't a leg. That's a head."

"It isn't supposed to be a head," replied Neddie. "It's supposed to be a leg."

"Save it for the head," Betsy called out.

"All right," said Neddie. "Where shall I put it?"

"Roll it over here," said Betsy. "Here, where we're going to put the snowman."

Neddie rolled it to the spot Betsy had pointed at, but he had to roll it quite a long way. By the time he got it there, it was twice as big. When Betsy saw it, sh said, "That head is too big!"

Susan stopped to look at the head. "It can be the body," she said.

"It's too little for the body," said Betsy.

"It's too round for the leg!" shouted Neddie. "It's too big for the head! It's too little for the body! Isn't it good for anything?"

Betsy looked at it. Then she said, "Roll it some more and make it bigger. Then it will be big enough for the body."

"Okay," said Neddie, pushing the ball of snow again. "There is a lot of nice smooth snow up on that little hill." He pointed to a slope that ran from the front lawn up to the garden. Neddie found it hard work to push the big snowball up the hill. "Hey, Susan!" he called. "Come help me."

Susan came around from the side of the house and helped Neddie push the big ball up the hill. Then Susan looked at Betsy, and said, "What are you making, Betsy?"

"I'm making the head," Betsy replied.

"No, Betsy! I'm making the head!" said Susan.

"I thought you were making a leg," said Betsy.

"Well, I was," replied Susan, "but it got too round. So it can be the head."

"Oh!" said Betsy. "Well then, I'll make a leg."

"I thought Neddie was making a leg," said Susan. "That ball of Neddie's is much too big for a leg."

"He *was* making a leg," Betsy replied, "but it got too round so he made it into a head."

"But I have a head all made now," said Susan. "We don't want two heads. We want two legs."

"I know," said Betsy. "Neddie is making the body out of the head that was the leg."

"How many legs have we got?" asked Susan.

"We haven't any legs," said Betsy, "but I'm going to make a leg right now."

Susan went back to her work. Betsy began to shape her ball into something that looked more like a football. Meanwhile, Susan scraped off the sides of her round ball, making it into an oblong chunk. When she finished, she carried it in her arms over to Betsy and laid it down. Betsy said, "What's that?"

"It's a leg," said Susan.

"I thought you said you were making the head," said Betsy.

"You said we had two heads," replied Susan.

"No, I didn't," said Betsy. "I said we didn't want two heads."

"I know we don't want two heads," said Susan. "But if we don't have any head at all, how can we have two heads?"

Betsy explained. "I was making a head," she said. "Then you said you were making a head. Then I said we didn't want two heads, so I made a leg instead."

"Well, okay!" said Susan. "We have to have two legs, don't we?"

"Of course!" said Betsy.

"Well, here they are!" said Susan. "Two legs!"

Susan stood her leg on one end, and Betsy stood her leg up right beside it. "They are good legs," said Betsy.

"They have to be strong to hold up the body," said Susan.

"That's right," said Betsy.

Just then Neddie shouted, "Here comes the body!" Neddie gave the big ball of snow a push from the top of the hill, and it started to roll down. As it came, it gathered speed. It rolled past Betsy and Susan, knocked over the snowman's legs, and broke into pieces against the trunk of a tree.

Neddie came running and tumbling after it. "Why didn't you stop it?" he cried.

"Well, why did you let it roll down like that?" said Susan. "Just look at the snowman's legs!"

"Yes," said Betsy, "all squashed!"

"Where's his head?" said Neddie.

"He didn't have any head," replied Betsy.

The three children sat down in the snow

104

and looked at the wreck of the snowman. Their cheeks were bright red from working so hard. "I think it's too hard work, building a snowman," said Neddie.

"I guess we couldn't lift the body onto the legs anyway," said Susan.

"And we couldn't reach high enough to put the head on," said Betsy. "I guess we'd better wait until Father comes home. He'll help us."

Star came out of the front door. "Where is the snowman?" she asked.

"He didn't get born yet," replied Neddie.

While the children were resting, Thumpy was standing by an evergreen bush, barking at it. "I wonder what Thumpy is barking at," said Susan.

"He sees something in that bush," said Betsy.

"I wonder what it is," said Neddie.

The three children got to their feet. Betsy took hold of Star's hand, and they all walked over to the bush. They peered into the bush. "What is it, Betsy?" Star asked.

"I don't know yet," replied Betsy.

Neddie moved nearer. Then he pointed into the bush, and said, "There's a bird in there. It's a red bird. Like that cardinal bird that was on the roof."

"Where?" said Susan.

"Right in there," said Neddie, pointing. "Sort of in the back."

"Oh, yes," said Susan. "See, Betsy? It's bright red."

Betsy looked into the bush. In a moment she said, "I see it! I guess it's the cardinal." Then she said to Thumpy, "You leave that bird alone, Thumpy!"

"It's awful still," said Neddie. "It's not a bit scared of Thumpy."

"I wonder why it doesn't fly away," said Susan.

"See, Star?" said Betsy, pointing into the bush. "See the red bird?"

Star looked and said, "Oh, yes! I see it!"

"It doesn't move," said Betsy.

"Maybe it's frozen stiff," said Neddie.

"Birds can stand terribly cold weather," replied Betsy. "Our teacher told us all about birds."

"I'll bet it's dead," said Neddie.

"It is not dead!" said Betsy.

"How do you know?" said Neddie.

"It's an awful funny shape," said Susan. "It doesn't have any head."

"I guess it has its head under its wing. That's the way birds sleep," said Betsy.

"It couldn't sleep with Thumpy making all that noise," said Susan.

Just then Thumpy ran under the bush. "Thumpy, leave that bird alone!" cried Betsy. Betsy dove under the bush to catch Thumpy, but Thumpy was too quick for her.

"He's caught it!" cried Susan.

"He's got it!" cried Neddie.

"Drop it, Thumpy!" shouted Betsy. "Drop it!"

Thumpy did not drop it. Instead, he carried it in his mouth right to Betsy. Red feathers were sticking out of both sides of Thumpy's mouth. Betsy stooped down and held out her hand.

"Is it dead?" said Neddie.

Betsy looked at what Thumpy had laid in her hand. "Why, it isn't a bird at all!" said Betsy.

"What is it?" said Susan, leaning over to look.

"Let me see," said Neddie, pushing Susan aside.

"What is it, Betsy?" Star asked.

"Why, it's Clementine's red feather hat!" said Betsy.

"Is it hurt?" asked Susan.

Betsy smoothed the red feathers. She looked at the veil. It wasn't even torn. "It's all right," said Betsy. "Even the diamond is still there."

"Thumpy should get a reward for finding Clementine's hat," said Neddie.

"Let's go inside and give him a puppy biscuit," said Betsy. "Then we can take the hat over to Clementine. She'll be glad to see it. It's her best hat, you know!"

The children went into the house by the back door. Betsy's mother was in the kitchen. "Look, Mother!" Betsy cried. "Look what we have! Clementine's hat!"

"Where did you find it?" her mother asked.

"Thumpy found it," said Neddie. "It was on a bush."

"We're going to give Thumpy a puppy biscuit," said Star.

"It's Thumpy's reward," said Neddie. "Maybe we'll get a reward when we take the hat over to Clementine."

"Oh, Neddie!" said Susan. "You mustn't expect a reward. You didn't do anything."

"Clementine makes big ginger cookies almost every Monday morning," said

Betsy, "but we mustn't all go over with Clementine's hat."

"Why not?" said Susan. "We don't know for sure that she is making ginger cookies."

"No," said Neddie. "We're not going on purpose to get a ginger cookie. We're taking her hat to her."

"Mother," said Betsy, "what do you think?"

"It all depends upon your reason for going," replied her mother. "If you are going to take Clementine's hat to her, that's fine. If you are going for ginger cookies, that's not fine."

"We're going to take the hat," said Betsy and Susan and Neddie in a chorus.

Star felt that she had to say something too, so she said, "Yes!" and nodded her head very hard.

"Very well," said her mother. "See that you don't stand around waiting for ginger cookies."

"Oh, no! We won't!" said Betsy.

Betsy's mother put Clementine's hat into a brown paper bag, and the four children set out for the Jacksons' house. The sidewalks had been cleared of the heavy snow, so Betsy pulled Star on her sled.

110

Star held the bag with Clementine's hat on her lap.

When the children reached the Jacksons' house, they went to the back door. Betsy knocked on the door. In a moment Clementine's face looked out at the children through the glass in the upper part of the door. When she saw them she smiled her big, wide smile and opened the door. "Hello!" she said. "Come right in."

The children stepped into the kitchen. A delicious odor filled the room. It was the odor of ginger cookies. "Mmm! Something smells awful good," said Neddie. Susan gave Neddie a little kick on his shins.

"Ginger cookies," said Clementine.

"Clementine!" said Betsy. "Guess what!"

"I couldn't," said Clementine. "What?"

"Here's your best hat," said Betsy. "Thumpy found it hanging on a bush."

"Hanging on a bush!" cried Clementine. "Oh, my! Oh, my! I guess it's ruined. My beautiful red feather hat!"

"No, it isn't, Clementine," said Betsy, handing her the bag. "It isn't hurt a bit. You open the bag."

Clementine opened the bag and pulled out her hat. Her face was one big smile as she looked it over very carefully. "Well, now! What do you know!" she said. "Even the dewdrop is here."

Susan looked at the ginger cookies that were spread out on a white cloth on the kitchen table. She thought she had never seen such beautiful ginger cookies.

Clementine said, "I suppose you all like ginger cookies?"

"Oh, uh, not very much," said Susan. Now Neddie kicked Susan.

"I guess you never tasted good ones," said Clementine. "Just try mine!"

Just then Lillybell came into the kitchen. "My mommy makes the best ever," she said.

Clementine handed each of the children a big ginger cookie. The children all said, "Thank you, Clementine."

"And take one for Thumpy," said Clementine, as the children were leaving. "It's Thumpy's reward!"

The four children said good-by to Clementine and Lillybell. Betsy carried Thumpy's reward, and Susan pulled Star on the sled.

By the time the children had reached the corner, they had eaten their cookies.

112

"That's the best ginger cookie I ever tasted," said Neddie.

"Um! Yes!" said Susan.

"Does Thumpy like ginger cookies, Betsy?" asked Neddie.

" 'Course he does," said Betsy.

"Which does he like best, ginger cookies or puppy biscuits?" said Neddie.

"He likes them both," replied Betsy.

"But which does he like best?" said Neddie.

"I don't know," said Betsy.

"I guess he likes puppy biscuits best," said Neddie. " 'Cause if I were a dog, I would like puppy biscuits best."

"Yes, I guess so," said Betsy.

"Do you think he would like it if we gave him a puppy biscuit instead of that ginger cookie?" said Neddie.

Betsy thought about this. Then she said, "I don't know about that. Clementine gave this ginger cookie to us to give to Thumpy."

"I guess it wouldn't be fair if we didn't give it to him," said Susan.

"But we should be kind to animals," said Neddie. "If Thumpy likes puppy biscuits better than ginger cookies, we would be kind to him if we gave him a puppy biscuit instead of a ginger cookie." When Neddie finished this long speech, he was out of breath.

"Well," said Betsy, "I guess so." Betsy stood still. Susan stood still and the sled stopped. Neddie, Susan, and Star watched as Betsy broke the last ginger cookie into four pieces. "We're stealing from Thumpy," said Betsy.

"No, we're not!" said Neddie. "We're being kind to animals."

Chapter 8

Christmas Presents

By Monday evening Betsy's mother and
Mrs. Byrd were both feeling very happy.
The freezer, full of food, had begun to hum
again, and the lights went on. The telephone had rung, and Mrs. Byrd, Neddie,

and Susan had talked to the children's father and later to their grandmother. Betsy's father had found out where his car was, as well as Mrs. Byrd's. They had both talked to the man at the garage. Mrs. Byrd's car, he had said, would be ready on Wednesday, late in the afternoon.

When Betsy heard this, she said, "Oh, dear! I don't want you to go home. I thought you would be here for Christmas."

"We couldn't have Christmas without Daddy!" said Neddie.

"We have to do our Christmas shopping," said Susan.

"So do we," replied Betsy.

"When will we go to see Santa Claus?" asked Star.

"Perhaps I can take you tomorrow," replied her mother.

But that night it did just what the weatherman had said it would do. It snowed again. When the children woke up, it was snowing very hard. Snow hung on the trees. It fell into the orange-skin cups on the birds' Christmas tree. The peanut butter was covered with snow. During breakfast everyone listened to the radio. "Schools will be closed again today," said the radio announcer.

"No school! No school!" cried Betsy.

"What shall we do today?" Susan asked.

"We can look at television!" said Neddie. "It's working again."

"I think you had better start making your Christmas presents," said Betsy's mother. "Christmas is Friday, you know."

"That's only four days off," said Mrs. Byrd.

"How can we make our Christmas presents in such a short time?" said Betsy. "Aren't we going to go Christmas shopping?"

"We can't go out in this weather to do Christmas shopping," said her mother.

"But I have to get a present for my friend Ellen, and something for Billy Porter. Then there is Mr. Jackson and Mrs. Jackson and Lillybell and Clementine and Mr. Kilpatrick," said Betsy. "And lots of other people," she added, smiling at her mother. "You know who, don't you, Mother?"

"I think I do," said her mother, with a twinkle in her eye.

"I have to buy Christmas presents, too," said Susan.

"I don't know when you will be able to go out shopping," said Mrs. Byrd.

"Why don't you children spend today seeing how many presents you can make?" said Betsy's mother. "Suppose you lived far, far away from any stores. What would you do for Christmas presents?"

"You mean out in the wilderness?" asked Betsy.

"That's right," said her mother. "There is no place to buy anything in the wilderness."

"Do we live in a log cabin?" asked Neddie.

"Oh, yes!" said Betsy. "Let's live in a log cabin."

"Don't we have any automobile?" asked Neddie.

"Of course not!" said Susan.

"Not even a horse?" said Neddie.

"No horse," said Betsy. "We're poor."

"Don't we have any money at all?" asked Neddie.

"No money for Christmas presents," said Susan.

"I guess we won't get very many Christmas presents," said Neddie. "We're too poor."

"We'll be lucky if we each get one present," said Susan.

"Maybe we won't get any present at

all," said Neddie. "Maybe Santa Claus won't be able to come, because it's snowing so hard."

Star's face puckered up and she began to cry. "I want Santa Claus to come," she said.

Betsy put her arm around her little sister to comfort her. "Don't cry, Star," she said. "Santa Claus will come."

"How do you know he will?" said Neddie. "The roof is so slippery he won't be able to park his reindeer and his sleigh."

"That doesn't make any difference to Santa Claus," said Betsy. "He *always* comes. Come on, let's help Santa Claus. Let's make presents."

"How?" asked Neddie.

"There is a big box up in the storeroom," said Betsy. "We call it the patch box. We can use anything in the patch box, can't we, Mother?"

"Yes, you can," replied her mother. "Run along. Here are the scissors and glue. You always need them."

Betsy took the scissors and Susan took the glue. The children climbed the stairs to the third floor. At the head of the stairs Betsy opened a door. The children walked into a small room. Against the walls of the room, there were piles of boxes, trunks, suitcases, and hatboxes. There were several old chairs with broken seats and a chest of drawers. There was a cot, a rolled-up mattress, and a big mirror with a crack in it. Betsy knelt down in front of a large wooden box. "This is the patch box," she said.

Susan knelt down beside Betsy, and said, "Can we have anything at all?"

"We can have anything we can use," replied Betsy.

Neddie leaned over and looked into the box while Betsy and Susan rummaged through the contents. They pulled out things that they thought they could use and put them on the floor. The girls were delighted when they found a box filled with colored beads. The strings were broken and the beads were all mixed up. There were big beads and little beads, red beads, blue beads, green beads, striped beads, and spotted beads. There were gold beads and pearl beads. Susan said, "I hope I can find enough pearl beads to make a necklace for my mother."

"And I'll make a necklace of red ones for Clementine," said Betsy. "It will look nice with her red feather hat."

Neddie looked into the box of beads with a very glum face. "What am I going to make for Daddy?" he asked. "I can't make a string of beads for him. He has to have a necktie for Christmas."

"You're not looking, Neddie," said Betsy. "That's the trouble."

"You're not using your imagination," said Susan. "You have to use your imagination."

Neddie dug around in the patch box. He kept saying, "That's no good! That's no good!" Finally he said, "There isn't any necktie here! There isn't any necktie for Daddy!"

"Neddie," said Susan, "if there was a necktie, you wouldn't have to use your imagination."

"I can imagine a nice necktie for Daddy," said Neddie, "but I can't make one for him. If there isn't any necktie, then there isn't anything for Christmas for Daddy."

"There are other things besides neckties, Neddie," said Betsy.

"What?" said Neddie.

"Well, uh. Well," said Betsy, "why don't you string some beads for your mother?"

"Don't want to string beads for Mommy," said Neddie. "Want a Christmas present for Daddy." Neddie went back to hunting in the box. He dug down into the bottom of it and pulled up a long strip of bright red felt. "Hurrah!" shouted Neddie. "I've got a necktie for Daddy!"

Susan and Betsy looked at the long strip of red felt hanging from Neddie's hand. "That doesn't look a bit like a necktie," said Susan.

"No, it looks like a belt," said Betsy.

"Okay, it's a belt for Daddy," said Neddie.

"It can't be a belt," said Susan, "because it hasn't any buckle."

"Well, I like it anyway," said Neddie, sitting down on the floor beside Star.

Star was busy looking through a pile of old Christmas cards that she had emptied out of a big shopping bag. Every once in a while, she would hold one up and say, "Look! Pretty!" Neddie began to look at the Christmas cards too. As Star laid each one down, Neddie picked it up.

Suddenly Neddie had an idea. He began cutting the long strip of red felt into small strips. Each piece was about six inches long and about an inch wide. Soon Neddie

had quite a pile of strips of red felt. By the time he cut the whole piece into little strips, he had two dozen pieces. Then he set to work, cutting up the Christmas cards. He cut out Santa Claus heads. He cut out angels. He cut out stars and wreaths of holly. Neddie glued a picture to each piece of red felt.

When Susan finally looked over to see what Neddie was doing, he had a lot finished. "Neddie," she said, "what are you doing?"

"I'm using my imagination," replied Neddie. "I'm making bookmarks for Daddy."

Betsy leaned over and picked up one of the bookmarks. "Aren't they pretty!" she said.

"There will be a lot of bookmarks," said Susan. "Will you let Betsy and me have some of them, Neddie?"

"I'll give one to Mr. Jackson and one to Mr. Kilpatrick," said Betsy.

"And I'll give one to your father, Betsy," said Susan.

"They are my bookmarks," said Neddie. "I thought it up all by myself."

"That is very selfish of you, Neddie," said Susan.

"Well, uh," said Neddie, "I'll tell you what."

"What!" said Susan and Betsy, in a chorus.

"I'll sell you some," replied Neddie. "I'll have a store. Betsy said this is a storeroom, so I'm going to have a store."

"Oh, Neddie!" exclaimed Betsy. "That's a good idea. If we have a store, I can sell strings of beads."

"And I can sell bracelets," said Susan.

"Everybody can do their Christmas shopping," said Betsy.

"I thought of it," said Neddie, "with my imagination."

"Let's have lots of things," said Susan, returning to the patch box.

Susan and Betsy began to dig into the box again. They found more and more things that they could use to make Christmas presents. Betsy pulled up a long piece of gold cord. In a button box the girls found some gold buttons. They sewed the buttons all around the gold cord and made bangle bracelets.

Susan found a piece of bright blue leather. She made circles on the leather by drawing around the lid of a box. With the scissors, she cut on the lines.

"What are they for?" Neddie asked.

"To put under glasses of water, so they don't make marks on the table," replied Susan.

"You mean coasters," said Betsy.

Later Susan found a bunch of old socks with holes in the toes. She set to work immediately, cutting bigger holes in the toes. Next she cut up the lid of a red cardboard box into small pieces. She folded each piece in half and stuck it into the hole in the sock. Then she sewed it fast to the sock. When Susan had finished, she slipped her hand into the sock and called out, "Look!"

Betsy and Neddie and Star all looked at Susan. Susan held up the sock and opened and closed the piece of red cardboard. It looked just like a mouth. "This is going to be a puppet," she said. "All I have to do now is sew some buttons on for eyes."

"That's great!" said Neddie.

Betsy held up a scrap of black fur. "You can sew this on for hair," she said.

"Oh, Betsy!" exclaimed Susan. "You have the best imagination."

By the end of the day, there were a lot of Christmas presents sitting around the storeroom. "When shall we have the store and sell our things?" Neddie asked.

"After dinner, I guess," said Betsy. "Before we go to bed."

"Who will come to buy in the store?" said Neddie.

"We all will," replied Betsy. "And your mother and my mother and father will come to do their Christmas shopping, too."

"Well, I won't have time," said Neddie, " 'cause I have something else to do."

"What?" asked Betsy.

Neddie made a funny face, and said, "It's a surprise. I thought it up with my imagination."

At dinner the children told the grownups about their store up on the third floor. Betsy said to her father, "We made a lot of Christmas presents, Father. I hope you will be a good customer."

"I hope the prices are not too high," said her father.

"Oh, no," said Betsy. "Nothing over twenty-five cents."

As soon as dinner was over, Neddie ran to the hall closet. "Don't anybody come until I call *ready*," Neddie called back.

"Okay," said Susan and Betsy.

They heard Neddie run up the stairs. Then they heard him running around in Star's room. They heard the closet door open and shut. Then they heard him running up the third-story stairs. Before long they heard Neddie shout, "Ready!"

Everyone went upstairs. When they walked into the storeroom, they found a counter made of an old ironing board stretched between two chairs. Strings of beads and bracelets lay at one end of the counter. Some puppets, brown ones and black ones, lay at the other end, with their red mouths gaping open and their eyes staring up at the ceiling. There were pot-holders made of braided bags and there were blue leather coasters. There was a whole pile of Neddie's bookmarks.

Everyone looked around for Neddie. Neddie didn't seem to be there, but sitting on a rickety, old chair was someone who looked like a little Santa Claus. Of course, everyone made believe that they didn't know who it was, but even Star knew that it was Neddie. He was wearing his red bathrobe and his black galoshes. On his head he was wearing Betsy's red hood from her snow suit. There was white cotton sticking out all around the hood, and

he had a white cotton beard. His head looked as though it had been laid away in a box filled with white cotton.

"Come, boys and girls!" he called out. "Come shake hands with Santa Claus." Everyone shook hands with Santa Claus, and told him what they wanted for Christmas.

Betsy and Susan did the selling, but they did some buying, too. Before long, the money was all mixed up. Santa Claus did some buying also, and the money got mixed up more than ever. When it was time to go to bed, the children decided to divide the money evenly, because they were too tired and sleepy to straighten everything out.

Everyone went to bed satisfied with the results of their Christmas shopping. After Susan and Betsy were in bed, Susan said, "Betsy, are you asleep?"

"No," replied Betsy.

"We don't live in the wilderness, do we?" said Susan.

"No, not for real," Betsy replied.

"You do think our mothers and fathers will give us something for Christmas that they didn't buy in our store, don't you?" Susan asked.

"I hope so!" said Betsy.

Suddenly Neddie appeared. "Susan!" he said. "Susan!"

"What's the matter, Neddie?" said Susan.

"I don't want a bookmark for Christmas," he said. "I want a dog like Thumpy. You don't think Mommy bought a bookmark for me, do you? The bookmarks are for Daddy. I want a cocker spaniel."

"Well, go to bed, Neddie," said Susan. "Maybe Santa Claus will bring you a cocker spaniel like Thumpy."

"I sure hope so," said Neddie.

Chapter 9

Secrets

On Wednesday morning the world was bright with sunshine, but many roads were still blocked with snow. The schools were closed for the third day. "I'm sorry there isn't any school today," said Betsy at breakfast. "Because today we were going to have the Christmas program."

"Yes," said her mother. "Christmas vacation begins tomorrow."

"It's a long vacation this year," said Betsy.

"Maybe it will snow some more after Christmas is over," said Susan, laughing. "Then you won't have to go back to school."

"Yes," said Neddie. "Maybe you won't have to go back to school until the Fourth of July!"

"Silly!" said Susan. "Nobody goes to school on the Fourth of July." The children laughed.

They played in the snow almost all morning. Just before lunch, Betsy's mother and Mrs. Byrd came out of the house. They were both bundled up in their warmest clothes. "Come, children," said Betsy's mother. "Let's all walk to the grocery store."

"Can we take the sled?" asked Betsy.

"Yes," said her mother. "We can put all the groceries on the sled and pull them home."

"Can I ride to the store on it?" Star asked.

"We'll take turns," said Betsy. The children took turns riding on the sled to the grocery store. They were not very anxious, though, to take turns pulling the sled home again. The box of groceries was heavy.

When the children and their mothers reached home, there was a telegram sticking out of the mailbox. "Oh, look!" said Betsy. "Here's a telegram!"

Betsy pulled it out and handed it to her mother. Her mother looked at the envelope and gave it to Mrs. Byrd. "It's for you," she said.

"Thank you," said Mrs. Byrd. She tore the envelope open. Susan and Neddie watched while their mother read the message. They saw her smile. Then she said, "Daddy is coming!"

"When?" the two children asked.

"Today," replied their mother. "This afternoon. He will drive us to Grandmother's."

"Today!" exclaimed Betsy. "Not today!"

Mrs. Byrd laughed and put her arm around Betsy. "It's sweet of you, Betsy, to be sorry to have us go," she said.

"We are all sorry," said Betsy's mother.

"So near Christmas, too!" said Betsy.

"But we must go to Grandmother's," said Mrs. Byrd. "She expected us last Friday. We were going to drive her back to our house for the Christmas holidays. Now we shall have Christmas with her, instead of Granny having Christmas with us."

"Your car won't be ready until five o'clock," said Betsy's mother. "You will all have dinner here with us, won't you?"

"That will be nice," replied Mrs. Byrd, "but we shall have to leave right after dinner to get to Granny's before midnight."

"What time will Daddy be here?" Susan asked.

"He's coming on the train," replied her mother. "He didn't say what time it arrives."

"How will he get here from the station?" asked Neddie.

"He will come in a taxicab, I suppose," said his mother.

"I can't wait for Daddy to come," said Neddie. "Do you think he will bring our Christmas presents with him?"

"I don't know about that," his mother replied.

"I guess he couldn't bring what I want," said Neddie. "I guess he wouldn't be able to bring a cocker spaniel with him."

It was hard for Betsy to believe that the time had almost arrived for the Byrds to leave. She and Star and Susan and Neddie had had such fun together. Now it would soon be time for them to go, and she did not have the presents for them that she had been thinking about. She knew she would have to make them this very afternoon.

As soon as lunch was over, Betsy slipped away from the other children. First she went down to the laundry and got the bottle of wash bluing. Then she went up to the bathroom and locked the door. Susan and Neddie were watching at the front window for their father, so they didn't miss Betsy.

Lillybell had come to play with Star. It wasn't long before they discovered where Betsy was. Star knocked on the bathroom door, and called, "Betsy! Let me in. Betsy!"

Lillybell knocked on the door too, and called, "Betsy! Star wants to come in."

Betsy opened the door and both little girls came in. "What you doing?" Star asked.

"I'm making some doll slippers blue," said Betsy, locking the door again.

"Why?" asked Star.

"They are for Susan for Christmas," replied Betsy. "I heard her say she wanted a pair of blue slippers for her doll."

"Oh," said Star.

"The only doll slippers I have are white, but Mother said I could use some of this wash bluing," said Betsy. "It will make the slippers blue."

"Oh," said Star.

"Can we watch you?" said Lillybell.

"Yes, but don't tell Susan about the slippers," said Betsy. "It's a secret."

"We won't tell," said Lillybell.

"No!" said Star, shaking her head.

Betsy ran a little water into the washbasin. Then she poured some of the bluing into the water. It turned the water a deep blue. Next Betsy dipped the white canvas slippers into the blue water.

Star was too little to see over the edge of the washstand. "Are they blue now?" she asked.

"They have to soak a little while," said Betsy.

Star and Lillybell couldn't see the slippers, so they decided to leave. Betsy unlocked the door and the two little girls departed. They went downstairs, where they found Susan and Neddie sitting on the floor in the living room playing a game. "What you doing?" said Star.

"What you doing?" said Lillybell.

"We're playing Authors," said Susan.

"Oh," said Star.

"Where's Betsy?" Susan asked.

"She's in the bathroom," said Lillybell.

"She's making something blue," said Star.

"They're not blue yet," said Lillybell. "She has to let them soak."

" 'Cause they weren't blue enough," said Star.

"It's a secret!" said Lillybell.

"We can't tell a secret," said Star.

"No, we can't tell what Betsy is making blue," said Lillybell, " 'cause that's the secret."

Star and Lillybell didn't think it was any fun to watch Susan and Neddie playing Authors, so they went upstairs again. "Betsy!" Star called from outside the bathroom door. "Betsy, let me in."

Betsy unlocked the door, and Star and Lillybell came in. They saw that Betsy had some things on the bathroom floor. There was a jar of glue, a pair of scissors, and some papers. "What you doing?" said Star, as Betsy sat down on the floor.

"I'm gluing something," said Betsy. "I have to hurry."

"What you gluing?" said Lillybell, sitting down on the floor beside Betsy. Star sat down, too.

"It's a secret," said Betsy.

"Another secret!" said Lillybell.

"It's Neddie's Christmas present," said Betsy.

Betsy picked up a colored picture of a cocker spaniel. "Neddie wants a cocker spaniel for Christmas, so I'm going to make a jigsaw puzzle out of this picture of a cocker spaniel."

"Oh," said Lillybell.

"It looks like Thumpy," said Star.

"Can we watch?" Lillybell asked.

"Yes, but you mustn't tell," said Betsy.

"No! No!" said Star and Lillybell together.

The little girls watched Betsy as she pasted the picture of the cocker spaniel on a piece of cardboard. "Are you going to chop it all up?" asked Lillybell.

"Yes," said Betsy. "Then Neddie will have fun putting it together."

"Are you going to chop it up now?" Star asked.

"I have to wait for the glue to dry," said Betsy.

"Are the slippers dry?" asked Lillybell, scrambling to her feet. She went to the washstand. The little blue doll slippers were sitting on the edge of it. Lillybell picked them up. She was surprised to see that the soles of the blue slippers were still sitting on the washstand. "Oh, Betsy!" said Lillybell. "Look!"

Betsy looked. She saw that Lillybell was holding the tops of the blue slippers. Betsy jumped up. "Oh, dear," she said, when she saw the pair of tiny soles sitting on the washstand. "The water made the soles come off. Now I'll have to glue them back on." Betsy took the tops of the slippers from Lillybell. Then she set to work, gluing the tops to the soles.

"Let's go downstairs," said Star to Lillybell.

Betsy unlocked the door and said, "Now don't tell Neddie about the jigsaw puzzle. Remember, it's a secret."

"Yes, it's a secret!" said Star.

"Yes!" said Lillybell.

The little girls went downstairs again. Susan was alone. She was sewing. "What you doing?" said Star, as she came into the living room.

"I'm making a cape for Betsy's doll," said Susan. "What is Betsy doing?"

"She's gluing," said Star.

"What is she gluing?" asked Susan.

"Her shoes," said Star.

"Why is she gluing her shoes?" asked Susan.

"Because the bottoms came off," said Lillybell, "when they got wet."

"Did she go out in the snow without her galoshes?" said Susan.

"No," replied Star. "She wetted them in the washbasin."

"But why did she put her feet in the washbasin?" asked Susan.

"She didn't put her feet in the washbasin," said Lillybell. "It's a secret."

"Where's Neddie?" asked Star.

"He's in the cellar," replied Susan.

Star and Lillybell went to the cellar door in the kitchen. They opened the door and went down the stairs. They found Neddie looking around the cellar. "What you doing?" said Star.

"I'm looking for a basket for my puppy to sleep in. 'Cause Daddy might bring me a cocker-spaniel puppy for Christmas. He just might. I've got to have something for him to sleep in."

"Oh," said Star.

"Betsy has a pretty cocker spaniel," said Lillybell.

"I know that," said Neddie. "Thumpy."

"But she has another one," said Lilly-bell.

"Where?" said Neddie, stopping his search for a basket.

"Up in the bathroom," said Star. "She's cutting it up into little pieces."

"I don't believe it!" said Neddie. "You're making that all up."

"It's a secret!" said Lillybell. "You mustn't tell the secret, Star."

"I didn't," said Star.

Neddie was gone. He ran up the cellar stairs. Then he ran up the stairs to the locked bathroom door. "Betsy!" he called.

"Go away, Neddie!" Betsy called back. "Go away!"

"Have you got a dog in there?" Neddie shouted.

"Of course not!" replied Betsy. "Go away!"

At this moment the doorbell rang. Neddie almost fell down the stairs in his hurry to get to the front door. He reached it ahead of Susan. When Neddie opened the door, there stood his father.

"Daddy!" cried Neddie, flinging himself at his father's knees.

"Daddy!" cried Susan, rushing to him.

144

When Neddie let go of his father, Neddie found that his legs were tangled up in something that held him tight. He looked down, and there was a black cocker-spaniel puppy. His little leash was caught around Neddie's legs. "Oh, Daddy!" cried Neddie. "Is the puppy for me?"

"Yes, he's for you, Neddie," said his father, dropping an armload of Christmas parcels on the floor. "I had to bring him unwrapped. I hope you don't mind. Susan's present isn't alive, so it is wrapped."

Susan ran to find her mother, but Neddie just yelled as loud as he could yell, "Daddy's here! He brought me a cocker-spaniel puppy!" Everyone came running.

After the excitement was over, Susan and Betsy went off to wrap up their presents for each other. That evening dinner was early so that the Byrds could get on their way to their grandmother's. All during dinner Betsy's father and Mr. Byrd teased the children about the things they would get for Christmas. Everyone laughed a great deal.

As soon as dinner was over, the Byrd family began to get ready to leave. While they were putting on their things, everyone passed little Christmas parcels to each other. "This is for you! This is for you!" they kept saying. Betsy and Star and their father and mother were all sorry to see the Byrds go. They stood by the lighted front door and called to the Byrds as they walked down the snowy path to their car. "Good-by! Good-by! Merry Christmas!"

"Merry Christmas! Merry Christmas!" the Byrds called back.

Just as Betsy's father was about to close the door, Betsy remembered something. "Oh, Susan!" she called out. "You never showed us how to make angels in the snow."

"We shall have to come back someday," Mrs. Byrd called back.

Betsy's father closed the door. "Oh, dear!" sighed Betsy. "I did want to see an angel in the snow."

Outside, as the Byrds were getting into their car, Susan said, "I want to make an angel in the snow for Betsy. It won't take a minute."

"Very well," said her father, "but hurry."

Susan walked through the snow to a spot under Betsy's bedroom window. The snow was soft and without a single mark. Susan stood up straight with her arms spread out.

Then she let herself fall backward into the soft snow. When she was flat on her back, she moved both of her arms out and up, until her hands were high above her shoulders. Then, very carefully, she got up to her feet.

The next morning, when Betsy looked out of her window, she saw that the snow that had been so smooth was no longer unmarked. It looked as though an angel with spread wings had lain down in it. "Oh!" said Betsy aloud. "There's an angel in the snow!" She knew that Susan had made it for her.

ABOUT THE AUTHOR
AND ILLUSTRATOR

CAROLYN HAYWOOD is one of the most widely
read authors of books for children. Her first
story was " 'B' Is for Betsy," and she has since
written many books, twenty-six of them about
her two popular characters, Betsy and Eddie.
Also available in Archway Paperback editions
are *Eddie's Menagerie, Eddie the Dog Holder,
Eddie's Green Thumb, Betsy's Play School* and
Snowbound with Betsy.

Miss Haywood was born in Philadelphia,
Pennsylvania and studied at the Pennsylvania
Academy of Fine Arts. She won the Cresson
European Scholarship for distinguished work,
and became a portrait painter before she
started writing for children. She has illustrated
many of her own books.

Miss Haywood now lives in Chestnut Hill,
a suburb of Philadelphia.

A Dog in a Million!

Pete's best friend is Mishmash—a big, friendly dog who thinks he's human. Mish sleeps in a bed, eats at the table, and takes bubble baths. He hops into cars hoping for rides, adopts an imaginary playmate, and even gives a party for his dog friends!
Join Pete and Mishmash as they get mixed up in one hilarious adventure after another.

The MISHMASH books, by Molly Cone
Illustrated by Leonard Shortall:

_____	56083	$1.50	MISHMASH
_____	43711	$1.75	MISHMASH AND THE SUBSTITUTE TEACHER
_____	43135	$1.75	MISHMASH AND THE SAUERKRAUT MYSTERY
_____	43682	$1.75	MISHMASH AND UNCLE LOOEY
_____	29936	$1.50	MISHMASH AND THE VENUS FLYTRAP

133

ARCHWAY PAPERBACKS from Pocket Books